BONE

Also by Philip Terry

Poetry

Oulipoems

Oulipoems 2

Shakespeare's Sonnets

Advanced Immorality

Dante's Inferno

Quennets

Bad Times

Dictator

Turns

Fiction

Ovid Metamorphosed (ed.)

tapestry

When Two Are In Love or As I Came To Behind Frank's Transporter (with James Davies)

Translation

Raymond Queneau Elementary Morality

Georges Perec I Remember

The Penguin Book of Oulipo (ed.)

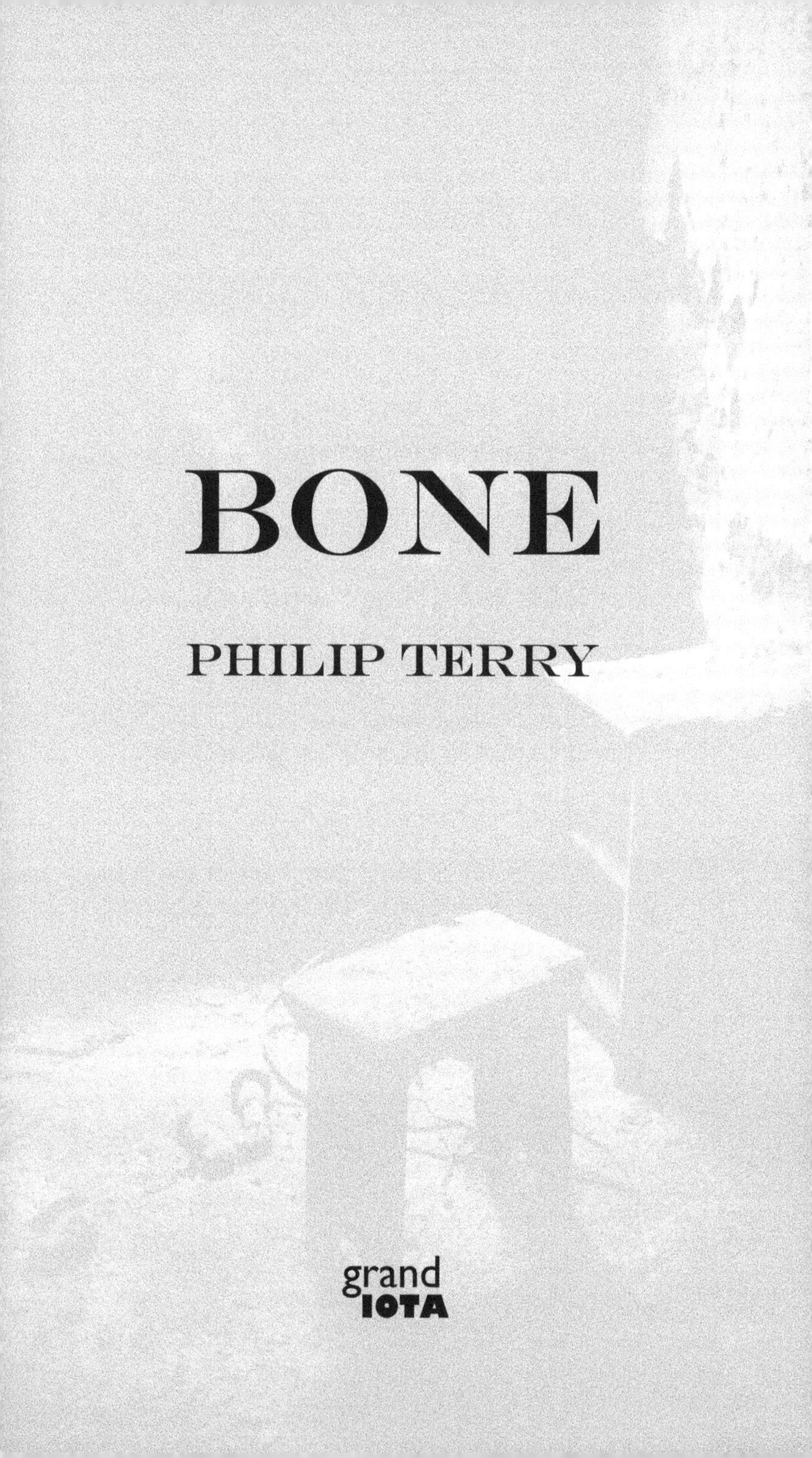

BONE

PHILIP TERRY

grand IOTA

Published by
grandIOTA

2 Shoreline, St Margaret's Rd, St Leonards TN37 6FB
&
37 Downsway, North Woodingdean, Brighton BN2 6BD

www.grandiota.co.uk

First edition 2021

Typesetting & book design by Reality Street

A catalogue record for this book is available from the British Library

ISBN: 978-1-874400-81-3

for Michèle Audin, who opened the door

When the swallow realised that emigration was the only possible life for her, she enlarged the muscles that worked her wings, and which became by degrees the most important part of her body. The mole went underground, and its whole body adapted itself to the task.

(Italo Svevo, *The Confessions of Zeno*)

I don't know what I'm here for, nor how I arrived. In a vehicle of some sort, I think, a van no doubt. Yet it could have been a car, who knows, even a sidecar. It could be that someone led me here on foot, I don't know. It could even be that I was carried here on horseback. But even here, where all seems feasible, instinct tells me not. I think I'd have remembered it, not with contentment, to be sure, for I'm no horse lover, but it would have stuck in the mind. Whatever, here I am, and it doesn't look like I'm here for the short haul.

Here. You couldn't, hand on heart, call it a room. More of a cell than a room. More of a cellar than a cell. But there's no wine, that should be obvious, at least not now. Better call it a cell then. Dimensions. It's difficult to tell in this blue-dark. Let's see. *See!* If I hold this old back of mine to the wall, in the corner, then stride forwards, I can take 1...2...3...oof!...three clear strides before I hit the other wall, hands outstretched. If I then rotate, don't rush, about 45° clockwise – no, 90° – and move backwards, a little bit, till this old back of mine leans once more on the cold wall, the other wall, or one of the other walls, then do the same manoeuvre once more, stride forward, hands outstretched, let's see...1...2...3...oofff!...same as before, more or less. The cellar then, or rather cell, is three strides and a bit in all directions. 10 ft x 10 ft, more or less.

*

The warder has been in. Told me to end the sorties around the cell. Nice to know someone's on watch. He has a little hole he can observe the cell from, and he's been told to check on me. Check I don't move. I asked him what was so bad about a brief walk round the cell, it's not as if I was about to make a run for it. Orders, he said. I didn't answer back. I sat down on the bed. Knees at 90°, elbows on knees, head between hands. I've been sat like this for some time now. Daren't move.

All of a sudden it struck me how odd it was that the warder could see me in here *at all* when he observed me from his little hole. I can't even see the wall on the other side of the cell, and I must be used to the dark. It's rare, so it is, dedication like that. Years of hard work, then in the end one can detect the merest twitch in total and absolute darkness. You'd think it would be easier to switch on a torch, but. Ours to reason it out. Is it to economise? Economise, black out the skies. Or could it be, on the other hand, that he has one of those infra-red devices? It's the hi-tech era, after all. He releases the catch over his little hole, sees a human-like blob of red strut about the room, arms out-stretched, as it makes a beeline for the solid stone wall. To do him credit, he could have felt inclined to do it for humanitarian reasons alone. Concern for the health of the inmate. After all, I wasn't hit, but told to end the sorties around the cell, that's all. Polite about it too. Whatever, looks like these sorties are out the window from now on. Have to devise some other amusements. Unless I can find a trick to tell when I'm watched. When not watched.

Where was I? That's it. Here for more than the *short haul*. But here where? No idea. No idea, either, for what reason I was taken here in the first instance. One minute I was free, the next? *Blam!* World out at the flick of a switch. After a while one starts to wonder what it's all about. After the initial shock. I was furnished with several accounts, or rather met with various accusations, which amounts to the same in the end, but none of it made much sense. I was taken down various dark and sinuous corridors into a room where a little man sat behind a wide table with an enormous book. He was flanked with two others, fatter and musclier than him. One of them he addressed as the Colonel, the other as the Lieutenant. It was this lot who furnished the accounts, made the accusations. The first was that I had crossed the border without authorisation. When I asked them which border the Lieutenant hit me across the face. I didn't ask a second time. Then the Colonel tied me to the chair, arms twisted into a knot round the back, and blindfolded me. The Colonel made further accusations, that I was a terrorist, a mole, a news columnist. I denied it all, as a matter of course. Besides, the Colonel was mistaken. One of them shouted at me – *"Whore! Slut!"* he shouted, his lexicon was rather limited – then another of them hit me across the face once more, but not as hard as on the first occasion, or so it seemed to me at the time. It could be that I was now so used to it all I didn't notice so much. I don't know. What's that maxim? Pain lessens with time? No, but that sort of idea. Pain lessens strain? No, but don't fret. Back on to that later, lock it in the store for when it rains. I know what I mean. Truth is there isn't a lot of rain to be seen here, nor a lot of sun either, in fact none whatsoever. Just a constant moisture in the air, and the smell of mould.

Later the Colonel came in with a document, and handed me a biro. Your confession, he said. I didn't read it. I couldn't. I still had the blindfold on. And even if I hadn't I don't think I would have read it. Whatever it said I was determined not to add a name to it. When I told them so the Colonel acted with calm. He could wait. It was academic, to tell the truth, he added. But I was threatened with torture if I continued to resist. If it was called for, the Lieutenant added, he could make me curse the hour I was born. He didn't indicate how. Just left it at that. For me to chew on, I think. Curse the hour I was born. That's how he couched it. Not what I'd call a clear statement of intent. Then I was led back here.

Time here moves in slow motion. There is little to see, no one to talk to, and nowhere to take off to. If I could knuckle down to some translation it would be the ideal time. But then I'd need a desk, some means to illuminate the cell, smokes, some food, a bottle of nice wine. What would I choose, now? A nice Chablis, that would do for a start. Don't want a wine that's too full-bodied. One to work with. Back at home, in the sun, I'm forever after the time to buckle down to some serious work, and all too often it's a battle I don't win, while here I have all the time in the world. I'd need a text too, of course. To translate. Oh, and some dictionaries, of course. Wouldn't do much without those. That manual for sailors I translated once. Such odd words! Some of them I'd never heard of before. What was it? The scutters. Is that it? No, that's from that round about drunken sailors. The one we used to chant in the car, on the road to Cornwall over the school vacation.

Put im in the scutters with a hose full on im
Put im in the scutters with a hose full on im
Put im in the scutters with a hose full on im
Earlie in the morrrn-in'!

Of course, I could translate the dimensions of the room. Into French, for instance. Trois mètres carrés. Not hard. What I need is some verse. A difficult verse. One from Yeats, for instance. William Butler. But I don't remember much but the sentimental ones, those he'd read on the radio in that loud, melodic voice of his.

I will arise and row now
And rooooow to Innisfreeee
And a small cabin buillld there
Of dum-de-dum and wattle maaaade

Can't even remember sufficient to make it worthwhile. And it wasn't "row now" I don't think. Print is such a Fascist at times. It drives out all memories till the brain's a tabula rasa. Even if mine wasn't all that fantastic in the first instance. I don't think the silence does much for it either. The darkness. Kind of smothers the mind. Like amnesia at times. There was that bit about the bee loud shade too, was that it? How did that run? Yes. *And live alooone in the bee loud shade*. Nice line that.

The time. From dawn to dusk. When the sun traverses the earth. Helios's chariot. It moves in slow motion. I must have said that before. Yet it is marked with a number of distinct events, nonetheless. The first event is at dawn, if we start with the dawn, which we need not do, but somehow it seems natural, even here, where nature has otherwise been abandoned. At dawn, then, the first event is when the coffee comes round. Not that the thin and flavourless brew that's dished out here much resembles what would be called coffee in the outside world. Coffee. Coffee. Doesn't fit somehow. The usual words don't work here, let's face it. But I have to make use of them all the same. It's all I have. The warder comes to a halt in front of the door and hammers on it with a metal cane. The noise is ferocious. *Krrraannnn! Krrraannnn!* This is the moment for me to fetch the mess tin, which is attached to a chain on the end of the bed. The man, for from the sound of his voice I think he must be a man, then uses a little hatch in the bottom of the door. I hear it click back, or slide back, one of the two, it doesn't much matter which. Soon as I can I make a beeline towards it and shove the tin out the other side of the hole. If I can find it. The hole, that is. There's a little shelf that sticks out on this side, near the base of the door, which facilitates this. I can feel it with an outstretched foot in the dark and once I've found it it's a doddle to locate the hole. Yet I can't dawdle. If I do he hammers on the door once more, and shouts at me. Move it woman! Move that fat arse over here now! That's what he shouts. Quite affectionate, I think. Once I've located the hole I shove the mess tin out and he fills it with coffee. The mess tin, not the hole. Then he sets it back on the shelf, from where I can retrieve it with ease. I think he must visit other cells before mine, for when the coffee reaches me it's more often than not cold. Yet of course, it could be deliberate. Just to show me who's boss. That wouldn't be unlike them. Whatever, I tend to drink it at once, for it fills the hole, the hole in the stomach, and it lines the aforementioned for the flavourless cooked oats which follow, cold, on its heels. Besides, if I didn't drink it I wouldn't have a vessel to stick the oat concoction in. For that's what's odd about the breakfast routine here, if I can call it a breakfast. Or a routine. That there isn't one vessel for the coffee, and another for the oats, but one vessel for both. So that no sooner have I located the hatch, shoved the mess tin in, had it filled with coffee, retrieved it and consumed it, the coffee not the mess tin, than I have to start the whole business over from the start. So as to have the mess tin filled with oats. And then when it reaches me at last, for the second time, the oats are stone cold. Perchance I've said that before. Taste of stale coffee too.

Then that's it till noon, when the broth ration comes round and is distributed in much the same fashion. The broth is most often lettuce and water, on the thin side, and like the coffee, when it reaches me it is more or less cold. Most often, it comes with a hunk of stale and mildewed bread. After this follow the interminable hours of the afternoon, tea, which most often consists of some kind of stew, and then the hours of dusk, with bed to follow. The hours between dawn and dusk are thus broken into two halves, that's how I see it at least, the end of the first half marked with the arrival of the broth. So far I can't tell which half is the most difficult to endure. Both have their bad and not so bad bits. The first half, which starts at dawn, finds me ravenous at the outset, but at least it has a clear and useful end. Dusk comes in on a relieved stomach, if not a full one, but its end is indistinct and therefore more remote.

Just started to scratch the old nose. Pick it, to call a shovel a shovel. It's difficult to do otherwise without a handkerchief at hand. I could blow it on a loose corner of these trousers, of course, but then I'd have to bend over, double in two more or less, and I could become stuck like that. Whatever, I started to scratch it, I know what I mean, and I was shocked to find how coarse the skin had become, round the corneal area above all, if that's the correct word. You could well wonder what made me feel round the corneal area, if I was minded to scratch the nose. So do I, now I mention it, but I was. There it is. Truth is odder than fiction, as it's often remarked. Well, I noticed that the skin had started to become rather coarse, like sandstone. Covered in hairs too, as if, like a man, I'd started to cultivate facial hair after all these barren decades. I don't think I'd be the first, however. What was the name of that Dutch noblewoman forced to tie the matrimonial knot when she had no desire to do so who willed herself to cultivate a beard? Power of the will. I could do with some of that. What should I cultivate? Mole-hands, to burrow out of the cell, burrow a tunnel under the earth then come out in the middle of a deserted field, miles from here. What was her name? Catherine? Isabella? Don't fret, I can't remember. I'd started to cultivate facial hair, like a man, that's what I'd started to think, when all of a sudden it occurred to me how daft I was. I still had the blindfold on. With both hands I eased it off, slow as I could, over the ears, over the nose, down over the chin, till it rested, loose, about the neck, like a scarf, or a noose. I felt the tired skin round the cornea with nervous hands. It was warm, smooth but for a few wrinkles, hairless.

Without the blindfold the room is still dark, but I can see it much better, nonetheless. What little illumination there is seems to come from a small and distant window fixed in the roof. It is black with filth, or soot, or ink, so that the illumination that infiltrates it has a dull, used, second-hand look about it. Yet it is sufficient for me to be able to make out a small sink, a foldable table without a chair, and a lone bucket that sits in the corner. The floor is hard and coarse, concrete I think, but it seems to have been laid in an uneven and hurried manner. It is cold and dank underfoot, fissured here and there with minute cracks, which start near the centre, then broaden and increase in size on their course towards one or other of the four walls, where these cracks come to a sudden halt. Some of the cracks, here, are of sufficient breadth to admit the entrance of a mouse, or a rat.

Peradventure it's in order to ward off such visitors that some of the cracks, where these meet the wall, have been stuffed with bits of old broadsheets, cloth, or hessian sacks. Yet it could also be to block off the entrance of air currents. Who shoved these materials into the cracks in the first instance, I wonder? If it was the warders, wouldn't it have been easier to have more concrete smoothed in? Would that not be at once more effective and more durable? Indeed, the overall unevenness of the concrete on the floor would lead one to think that this had been done before, several times even, and on cracks much wider than those now in evidence. Yet of course, one can't rule out the likelihood that their routine is to stuff the smaller cracks with old broadsheets, or bits of cloth, or hessian sacks, or whatever else is at hand, as a kind of interim measure, and then not until these become so broad as to render this means of renovation ineffective, to come back with the concrete. Which, after all, could have hidden costs and take a lot of time too.

Yet it could be that economics is not the sole factor at work here. It could even be that their aims are in some manner served via the use of these more makeshift means. To be sure, it adds to the sleaziness and overall sense of wretchedness. But then so would the rats, which in all likelihood these bits of old broadsheets, cloth and hessian sacks are there to ward off in the first instance.

Yet who can tell if the old broadsheets, cloth and hessian sacks were not left there with the intent to instil in the mind of the detainee, or in other minds, a fear of rats? For without a shadow of a doubt, it was when I saw these items, the old broadsheets, the cloth, the hessian sacks, that rats, or the idea of rats, first came to mind. For sure, I haven't seen or heard a sole rodent as it is. Devious. Well, if that's the case, then so be it. These arseholes can stuff their dumb tricks. And shove them into the inner recesses of their arses for all I care.

Yet what if it were a former inmate who for some reason or other had deemed it wise to stuff these holes with all this rubbish? For the rats, or for some other reason. Besides, it's hard to see how such rubbish would ward off rats, isn't it? Yet that wouldn't stand in the road of someone who wanted to have a bash. Would it? Where on earth would someone find the stuff in the first instance? To be sure, a fair amount of resourcefulness would be needed to find such stuff here. To find whatever kind of stuff here.

I've made a full search. There are no old broadsheets, cloth, or hessian sacks to be found. Save those hitherto stuffed in the cracks, of course. Which rules out the inmate theorem. Unless there were once old broadsheets and so on in the cell, and the inmate used it all in their endeavours. And it could be, with such limited resources, that the inmate felt inclined to stuff different cracks at different times. Such as for fluctuation of air currents due to alternations in exterior wind direction. When due south all old broadsheets, cloth, and hessian sacks to the north wall. When due north all old broadsheets, cloth, and hessian sacks to the south wall. When due east all old broadsheets, cloth, and hessian sacks to the west wall. When due west all old broadsheets, cloth, and hessian sacks to the east wall. And so on for north-west, south-east, north-east, and south-west. Not to mention north-northeast, east-northeast, east-southeast, south-southeast and the other half-winds.

It's not difficult to become carried off on a train of ideas like this in here. Pointless ideas soon breed in one's mind till one can't see the wood for the trees. If I've learnt one fact in this hole it is this. That multifariousness is not the salt but the actual stuff of life. If the reach of our minds is confined all of a sudden, we are often inclined to take the few items which offer themselves and ask a whole list of absurdities about them. So we set in train a ridiculous flow of combinations and associations in our minds, the duration and abstruseness of which soon obscure their humble foundation. I drove all ideas of old broadsheets, cloth, hessian sacks and air currents from the mind. Then I laid down on the bed, stuck the blindfold back on. If I hadn't, the warder, without doubt, would have done the same himself. Sooner or later.

*

Krrraannnn! Krrraannnn! That's the warder. It must be teatime. *Krrraannnn!* Quick as I can I crawl over to the door, before he starts to shout at me. Locate the shelf. Then the hole. Piece of cake, like I said. I shove the mess tin in. Then back it comes. Thin, tasteless stew, as usual. I bolt it down, as usual. Too much salt, for once. But no matter. A churl's feast is better than none at all.

I lie back in the dark, lids closed, hands at sides, limbs horizontal. Think about the situation. What it is. What the hazards are. How to better it. I know what these criminals are about. Or at least I think I do. I wasn't born last week. All their tricks are calculated to undermine one's free will. That's how I see it, as I lie back in the dark. Undermine one's free will. Get me to confess to some nonsense or other. That's what it's all about. I'm sure of it. 100%. Otherwise the bastards wouldn't do this to me. If there wasn't some hidden reason behind it all, let's face it, the Colonel could as well find me a room at the Ritz, or whatever else their nearest alternative is called, if there is one, the Rütz, the Rötz, the Rätz, whatever. I'd settle for a lot less, to be honest. A little illumination would be nice, to be sure, to fend off the darkness. And some music to ward off the silence, so as to remain in the land of the sane. Beethoven's trios, for instance. Deaf Beethoven. That's how he survived it all. Music. Could do it for me as well. And some modern stuff too, to alleviate the dullness. Some American music, for instance, like The Duke,

Thelonious Monk, those men, that would boost the morale a bit. As it is, all I have are these words. I daren't even voice them out loud, the warder would be in like a shot, and before I could mouth off a sentence he'd tie the muzzle back on. No. Don't want to risk that business all over. Mind, the warder could think I'd lost it in the end, think I was as mad as a hatter, and leave me to it. She's off on one this time, in there, he'd think, lost her marbles. First token of submission. Won't let them have the satisfaction. What is that maxim? Give him an inch and he'll take a mile. Well, he won't have even one of his inches out of me, that's for certain. Pinch an inch, that's another one, another remembrance. Where did I hear that? Pinch it from who? Or is it whom? Can't remember. Never mind. The words. These words. All I have now, and I can't even voice them out loud. Could be it's better like that, mine and mine alone. All mine. Freedom of the mind. Just hold them inside, let them run across the mind like water.

I'll soon run out of items to describe if I'm not careful. Still have the bed. The sink. Save them till later. Unless I'm moved to another cellar, another cell? That would be fun. Then I could run over it all for a second time. Dimensions, contents, materials, deliberations. Multifariousness. I need to introduce some multifariousness into life here. Some new hobbies. How did that character in Tolstoi do it? In that late tale about confinement. What was it called? He went on walks, walks of the mind, that was it. Made inventories of all he knew. You never know, I could have a bash too, couldn't I? Didn't he invent his own dialects too? I could do the same. Invent a new vernacular. Pack code, bonds the members. That's what the social scientists reckon, isn't it? But then there's but the one of me. Never mind, I'll have to be the whole band of sisters, I think, if it comes to that, a one-sister band. What shall I start with? What would be best, now? Writers. A list of writers. A-Z. To set on the invented bookshelf. Next to the table. Beside the wall. Do it!

Aristotle	
Balzac	
Chekov	
Dostoievski	But which one? *Crime and Punishment.*
Eliot	
Faulkner	
Gaskell	No, must be able to think of someone better. I know.
Goethe	
Hawthorne	
Ionesco	
James	Over nineteen stone he was. Sizeable, like his novels.

Kafka
Lear

Nietzsche
Ovid
Plutarch

Quevedo

The warder has been to see me once more. Took me to the other room. The one with the little man behind the wide table. I must have lost consciousness, and now I've come to I have a terrible skull-ache. The cross-examination was more focused this time. The Colonel had examined the I.D. I carried. Accused me of activities concomitant with those of a translator. That's what I have down on the I.D. No sin, as far as I can see. The Colonel chose to differ. Told me I was a subversive, a radical. I've tried to be, ever since I was born, I told them, didn't see what harm there was in it. There was a brief silence, then the Lieutenant unlocked the door and a broad, hard-nosed brute he addressed as Gore walked in. Gore carried a kind of truncheon in his left hand, thick and black with a nitid head, with which he beat the side of his trousers all the while. Wear a hole in them if he's not careful. We were introduced, then the Colonel carried on with the cross-examination.

Was it true what it said in the I.D., he asked? Yes, I said. And what kind of translation had I done? All sorts, I told them. Conferences, scientific texts, verse, news, adverts, business minutes, menus, novels and short stories, even a book of wisecracks once. Which hadn't been much of a success. In a word, whatever I had a commission to do, and sometimes I did non-commissioned work, if it interested me. Then the Colonel asked which idiolects. Idiolects?! Oh! I told them. Fluent in French and German, also skilled in Italian and Catalan. Basic Greek and Chinese. First "idiolect" Devonian. So I didn't disavow it? No, I said. Both the Colonel and the Lieutenant looked astonished. The Colonel chose this moment to leave his seat and held out a document to me. Quite ceremonious like. He held it in his left hand, while the other slid over his waistcoat, brushed over the medals, and eased a slim silver Sheaffer from inside his overcoat. He held this out as well. You must now authorise the confession, he said, with a smile. Pull the other one. More of a statement than an ask. No, I said. For what reason? retorted the Colonel, who was taken aback. Because I'm innocent, I said. The Lieutenant now left his seat as well, which made the little man in the middle look even littler, and motioned to Gore. One is often beaten about a lot in cross-examinations, but a skilled cross-examiner, it's said, will tend to ease off before the moment one loses consciousness. So the cross-examination can continue. In the end most cross-examinees confess. You'd have to be either a hero or a lunatic not to. That French lad the Nazis tortured in the war, in the "Free Zone". Returned to his mother's house without ears, teeth, nose, mouth or feature. He hadn't talked and would never talk from then on. Who knows, it could well have been that he had no crimes to confess in the first instance? I think I'd invent some before the cross-examiners went that far.

Gore came towards me and held his truncheon in the air, like a clockwork rozzer. He looked at the Colonel, who nodded. Then he hammered it down on the area of the skull with a dull thwack. *Krrrunkk!* I don't think he was a skilled cross-examiner, for I lost consciousness with more or less the first blow. If he loses his contract I won't shed a tear. It's no less than he deserves for this skull-ache he's left me with.

That list. The warder came to fetch me slam in the middle of it. Salt of life! Which damn letter did I reach? Ovid? Of course, I could start over from A, but I want to have a snooze, because of this bad head Gore's left me with. Start over from Ovid, then. What comes after that?

Plato
Quevedo
Ruskin
Stendhal
Tolstoi

Still can't remember the name of that tale.

Verlaine
Williams
Xenocrates

Yeats
Zola

Good idea that, the lists. Fills the time, and leaves one with the wholesome belief that a task, however small, has been done. Like when one does a crossword, or invents a new maxim. The streets of London are tarmacked with the old. Where did I hear that? Could invent some more in the same vein. A little collection to see out these hours of darkness. Leave a stain on the silence. I'll have to think of some. Sink or swim, as the cliché has it. Need to exercise the mind. I used to have the translation work to stretch me. Forever there whether I liked it or not. All those conferences, dossiers, news bulletins to read down the line. Forever on the old toes then. And the travel too. Berlin, Paris, Rome, Brussels, Amsterdam, London, Barcelona. I must have visited most of the main cities in the West at one time or another. Dwelt in a lot of them too. Got to earn a livelihood there and live like the natives. New York, as well, across the Atlantic. Yet I didn't have the chance to walk around much there. Americans don't like to walk much. Prefer taxis. I'll have to exercise the little sense I'm left with from the inside now, devise some new amusements.

*

Krrreennnn! Krrreennnn! OK, I'm on the case! *Krrreennnn!* Christ, that head of mine! The warder once more. Must be here with the broth and bread. Bound to have missed the breakfast. Quick, make sure the blindfold's on as it should be. In case he has a look. A look in his little hole. Now take the tin and crawl to the door before he starts to hammer on it. Quick. Now, where's the shelf? Oof! Got it. Now bend down, shove the tin into the hatch. That's it. He takes it from me in turn and I hear him ladle the broth in. This is the best moment. You hear it, but haven't tasted it. He shoves it back. At once I lift it off the floor, ravenous, like a hound. Then he shoves the bread in, which I stash at once. I'm now sat on the bed. Guzzle down the broth as fast as I can. Usual lettuce and water mixture. Salt taste this afternoon. Thin as bile water. There. None left now. As is usual, I'm still famished. He doles out sufficient to make one salivate, no more, and afterwards one is left even more famished than before. There's the bread, of course, but here too there's a catch. If one eats it at once, there's a chance one'll feel full for an hour or two, and this shortens the interminable wait till tea. But after that there are the endless hours of darkness that stretch out till breakfast. If one has eaten the bread at once this is when one wishes one hadn't. Survival in the hours of darkness without a bite to eat is no fun, take it from me. Often one wakes in the cold, and then can't do more than snooze on and off for what must be hours, and at such times a morsel of bread to chew on is a reliable calmative. It's for this reason that I often save it, difficult as this is. You have to be devious sometimes not to scoff it all at once. Sometimes I leave the bread on the shelf, and set some brain-teaser or other to finish before I'm allowed to touch it. Like calculate from a certain three-unit number, so as to finish with the number's cube.

$$101^2=10201$$
$$101^3=1030301$$

That's not a brilliant illustration. Often when I've finished I can't remember the number I started with, and in such cases I sometimes do the whole calculation in reverse. If the cube root isn't a three-unit number I know I've made a mistake somewhere, and then I start over. At other times I hide the bread under the mattress, then I do the best I can not to think about it; or I take a middle road, eat half of it and hide the other half. Pretend I've eaten it all. This method is less effective than the former, for some reason or other. Because it doesn't have a clear and fixed aim, I think. At times I can't remember what I've done and think I've hidden it all; then, when I retrieve it and find no more than half, I feel dissatisfied. At other times I can't hold back and ransack the cache in seconds.

This afternoon I've hidden it in a little crevice I found in the wall. Just to the left of the door. To be exact, it's more of a recess than a crevice. Yet whatever I call it doesn't alter its function, and it's this that matters, at least as far as I'm concerned. It serves me as a little nook where it's safe to store the bread, or whatever else I need to hide for a while, if I had other items I needed to hide for a while, which I don't. Yet one must continue to believe that better times lie ahead. It is about four inches across at the bottom, with a vault-like roof, and resembles the mouth of a small cave which has been cut into the coarse fetid stone out of which the cell is constructed. It seems reasonable to infer that a former inmate hollowed it out, for it bears the telltale hallmarks of a crevice that human hands have made. While its overall form is uneven from an aesthetic view, its floor has been rubbed smooth as if to offer a flat surface so that chattels can be slid in and out at ease. Also, its location shows a modicum of contrivance, for it is situated to the left of the door, so that when the warder comes in it will be concealed, if the door remains unclosed, which it often does. For whenever the warder comes in it is never for an extended time. It is either to fetch the inmate, or to tell her off, or to beat her, and none of these actions take much time to execute. So it is not worth his while to close the door. You could reason that he should do so all the same, to rule out a rush for freedom on the inmate's side, but this course of events does not seem to have occurred to him. Nor had it occurred to me, until now. Yet if I tried to make a dash for it I doubt I'd make a success of it. I don't even know for sure what lies on the other side of the door, I believe it must be a corridor of some sort. And, for sure, I don't have much sense of the fortress's architecture. In addition, when I was tracked down and thrown back in here there would doubtless be recriminations.

Jesus! This is all I need. I can't for the life of me find where it's located, the recess, now that I want to retrieve the bread. I know it's around here somewhere, to the left of the door. I search the stonework with bare hands, face close to the wall, I can feel the moisture, and the soft mould which has made its home here, acrid to smell. Where on earth is it now? What about over here, have I tried there? No. I'd better take the blindfold off. Take a chance. Otherwise I'll never find it. Hmmm. Let's see. Wait till the retina becomes accustomed to the dimness. Let's see now. Is that it? Yes. The little devil, so it is to the left of the door after all. Started to think I'd lost it there for a moment. Just a little more elevated than I remembered. At least the bread's still there. Take it out. Ahh!

Now the blindfold's off I'll finish the itemisation of the room and its contents. Get it over with, then on to fields anew. The illumination is faint, but it's sufficient to see with. I must've become acclimatised to the dark, like the warder. First the bed. It is next to one of the walls, more or less in the middle. It is a modest wooden bed, some five feet from head to toe, constructed of three coarse-hewn slabs of wood which run in line with the wall, fixed to a solid iron frame which is bolted to the floor. There is a straw mattress, a little on the thin side, and over this there are two coarse khaki blankets. No sheets. No bolster. Just next to the end of the bed, on the other wall, one of the other walls, is the sink. It is small and unclean with one lone and rather rusted faucet. If one turns this in an anti-clockwise direction it releases the water flow, which is more difficult than it sounds, because of the rust. When one succeeds the whole waterworks makes a severe metallic sound, which is horrific the first time, but which one soon becomes used to. That maxim. What one's used to can't do harm? No, I don't think so. Don't fret. Back on to that later. The faucet. It's a mistake to force it and turn it on in one decisive hand movement. It won't answer to brute force. The trick is to turn it ever so little in the chosen direction, that is, anti-clockwise, then turn it back in the other direction, that is, clockwise, a little less than before. If one does this over and over, and it becomes easier the more one does it, in fact the whole business can be carried out in a matter of minutes once one is used to it, the faucet answers in the end with a welcome mutter. The cold brown water which comes out in a dribble, then in a thin trickle, is small reward for all the effort, but this is all one has access to, so one has to make the most of it. Better one's hound muddied home than no hound at all, as is often remarked. If I was more on the ball at such times, I could fill the mess tin with water and leave it to stand for a while, till the sediment settled a bit, but it's difficult in the heat of the moment. Yet I could do that sometime nonetheless, if I remember. We'll see.

When I take a look at the sink I notice for the first time a tube of dentifrice. Perchance the warder left it there for me in the hours of darkness? If he did, he omitted to add a toothbrush. What brand it is I can't tell. Most of the letters have worn off, but for the letters L and E which are still visible, red on a whitish tube. I test it. The dentifrice is like cement, or rather crushed chalk, but still retains a faint flavour of mint, sufficient to mask the taste of the sour brackish water, nonetheless. Be thankful for small mercies.

I have an idea. If I stick a blob of dentifrice on this side of the hole I should be able to tell whether or not I'm under observation. I'll be able to see it when the hole's closed, like it is now, but when the warder disturbs it, to have a look in, the dentifrice will vanish. There, that should do it. It remains visible, even from the other end of the room. Shall have to wait a bit to see if it works. For the moment, as far as I know, I'm not under observation. If I'm mistaken, I'll soon hear about it.

I start to feel like a criminal sometimes when I execute these little acts of vandalism. I know I shouldn't, that this is how the Colonel and the Lieutenant, not to mention Gore, would like me to feel, but all the same that's what I feel. It starts as soon as one's locked in the slammer. What it's made for, no doubt. At such moments I start to root around in the shadowland of half-buried memories for some sinful secret, some diabolical misdemeanour. But there are no skeletons to be found in the closet, no bodies buried at the bottom of the orchard, no madwoman in the attic. The truth is that I have no secrets to hide. Which is not so unusual as all that. Yet this doesn't make it much easier in the end. I'm told I stand accused of treason, as a British mole. I tell them that's rubbish. This much is clear. Yet for one's cross-examiners such a denial constitutes in itself incontrovertible evidence of disobedience, and further convinces them that I have hidden secrets. That I work as a translator adds to their distrust. For to translate is to cross borders. To cross borders, for them, is a crime. Translation is also an indication of unwholesome and innate nosiness, and nosiness is the hallmark of the mole. Thus what in the world I know is considered normal, laudable even, is in theirs an indicator of crime. Put like this it sounds clear at least. It's a matter of two distinct worlds, mine and theirs, which share certain basic ideas, but in each the idea can indicate total antitheses. In the world I come from translation indicates skill, acumen, worldliness. In theirs it indicates nosiness, disobedience, mole-work, crime. Given that this is the case, I should not fall victim to bouts of self-doubt, that's what I have to hold on to. But it's no use. Guilt is a creature that roams the wilderness, outside of conscious control. That blob of dentifrice on the cell door hasn't benefitted me, for sure. If the warder finds it I'll be cross-examined, and when the Colonel accuses me of this act of defiance I won't be able to forswear it. Then I'll have to face the music.

Prison. To do time. That's what it's called, isn't it? More about what time does to the inmate, if one thinks about it. How to make the clock turn round with minimum discomfort, there's the rub. What the hobbies are for. Pastimes. Pass the time. Never noticed that before. Odd. What shall I choose then? What haven't I done? Inventories? Maxims? A walk? Yes, I feel like a walk most of all. Would revive me a bit too. Get out of here! Stretch the old limbs. Where then? Somewhere I know well, have to be. Could take Paris? Yes, Paris. Paris, which I love so much even if it has never treated me well. Around the Marais. Yes. I'm off.

I leave the rue Saint-Martin and meander onto the vast and treeless area beneath the now famous inside-out concretion that dominates the locale, the work of the architects Renzo Piano and Gianfranco Franchini. It towers before me, a colourful hi-tech warehouse of vitreous armour and steel, the blue of its air vents a shade darker than the blue of the heavens. Before me a band of fire-eaters, their tattooed forearms bathed in the afternoon sunshine, enact their stunts in front of a small crowd of adults and children. The crowd consists of about nineteen individuals, around ten adults and nine or so children, but its exact constitution alters from time to time as new onlookers arrive and others drift off. Further to the left an old man in a beret and blue overalls bends over a battered suitcase from which he extracts wooden annuli, a little ladder and a diminutive dais. He has three trained Chihuahuas which in turn he invites to somersault into the annuli, climb the ladder and stand on their hind feet on the dais. Once there each Chihuahua has its own trick to show off. One of them counts to thirteen with its tail, one barks out the Marseillaise while its master beats time with a tambourine, one balances a ball on its nose, throws it into the air, then catches it in its mouth. As I advance across the concourse, to flee the crowd, other street entertainers come into view. Acrobats, dancers, a one-man-band, comedians, mime artists. An accordionist with a Macaw on his shoulder, a lone bassoonist in a wetsuit with his instrument in a basin of water who blows out variations on Bal de Paris, two fiddlers in kilts with their children on flute and bodhrán, a violin trio dressed in tuxedos and bow ties who bow a Viennese waltz, a man dressed like Buster Keaton who does Blue Moon on a saw. There are also caricaturists, stands with art and souvenirs, vendors of waffles and ice-cream. Others distribute leaflets which invite tourists to come and listen to a celebrated instrumentalist at Saint-Eustache, some drummer at the Maison des Lombards, or an electroacoustic concert which features Karlheinz Stockhausen in the studios of IRCAM beneath our feet. All around, there is the crowd: some stand, some sit, others look at souvenirs, others stand in line, hands in their trousers, or noses in the air. Fine Art students with short hair wield their art folders and discuss that afternoon's courses, their ideas for later on. "Il vaut mieux aller chez Claude," someone offers. "Mais non, c'est chiant ça," another intones. There are businessmen in smart suits who make a dash for one of the area's bars or brasseries to take a lunchtime snack, a salade niçoise or steak-frites with a beer or a carafe of wine, before it's time for the next boardroom brainstorm; lovers who discuss their dreams for the future beneath the shade of trees; old men in berets who smoke their Gauloises on a bench and dream of boules matches at the seaside.

As I leave the concourse and the noise of the crowd behind me, I enter the rue Pierre-au-Lard, which dates from the C13th. Its successive names – Pierre-Allard, O'Lard, Pierrot, Père Ollier – are all deformations of the name Pierre Oilard, a Parisian merchant who once lived here. All around extends one of the most ancient districts of Paris, a maze of narrow streets whose bizarre names take one back to the secret heart of this historic area. Ahead lies the rue Sainte-Croix-de-la-Bretonnerie, which dates from around 1230, and whose name derives from an area once named the "Field of the Bretons" (where, it is said, five soldiers in the service of Edward I tried to assassinate the last leader of the Gauls), and from a convent of the name of Sainte Croix.

At an intersection of the rue Saint-Merri, I turn left, in front of the rue du Plâtre, on the other side, where Monsieur du Plastre, the inventor of Plaster of Paris, once had his home. Further on, on the left, I can see the rue le Franc, where, it is said, a counterfeit coin racket thrived in the C18th. When, a little further on, I reach the rue Rambuteau, I turn left once more, and leave the Marais, with its restaurants, bars, laundromats, hotels and delicatessens. The road is deserted, save for a few abandoned cars, an ownerless mutt, and an old drunk with a wooden limb who mumbles inscrutable words of solicitation as I come near. His teeth are black and his uncombed beard is matted with dirt. "La Résistance! La Résistance!" he mutters. "Foutou!" And once more. "C'est foutou la Résistance!" A bit of cord is tied around his neck, onto which have been threaded a number of discordant items: a carrot, several corks, used metro tickets, a small scale model of the Eiffel tower, and other curios whose exact nature it is difficult to determine. As I make haste to avoid his clutches, he hurls a crust of stale buttered bread at me, which misses its mark and hits a baker's window. While I leave the scene, I hear the voice of the owner hurl abuse at him. "Sale clochard!" she shouts. "Vous êtes de la merde!" The drunk mumbles a few words – "Excusez-moi madame, mais..." – and of a sudden all becomes calm once more. Perchance, in a lowered voice, he tells the irate owner that the woman in retreat in the short dark coat is the real offender, or that he acted in self-defence. Or it could be that when he sees all the multifarious cakes and croissants and delicacies in the window, he is dumbstruck – for this is a fine baker's, famed across Paris for its tarte de la maison, tarte aux fruits de bois. He stands there, in a drunken reverie, as in his vacant mind he devours the croissants, the brioches, the croissants aux amandes, the tartes aux fraises, the flans, and the unrivalled and delectable tartes aux fruits de bois....

A few moments later and I have come full circle. I see once more the acrobats, the fire-eaters, the musicians, the mime artists, the comedians, the dancers, the caricaturists, the vendors of waffles and ice-cream, and the old man in a beret and blue overalls who now stacks the wooden annuli, the little ladder and the dais in his battered suitcase. I take a seat on the terrace of a roadside café and make an effort to catch the attention of the waiter as he hurries hither and thither between the tables. In the interior of the bar three drunken Frenchmen intone misheard words to a well-known tune:

> If Hue toes down to zee woods to–dee
> Ee'd better look in zee skies (zee skies!)
> If Hue toes down to zee woods to flee
> He's in for a bee sore flies (sore flies!)
> For all zee bees zat ever zere was
> Is mustered zere for certain because
> To–dee's zee dee zee killer bees zave zeir fêêê—te!

The waiter arrives to take the order. “Un café crème et un verre d’eau merci,” I utter, in the best French I can muster, before he rushes off once more, to vanish into the interior of the bar. On the table someone has left a half-finished coffee, a half-full box of Gitanes, and a ticket that reads:

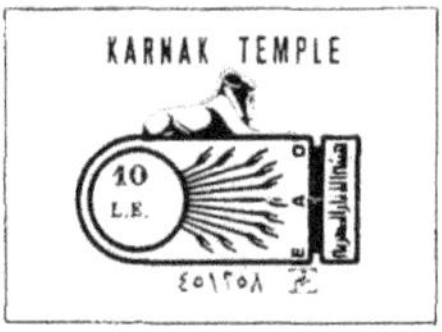

I am well aware that the tourist site of Karnak is not in Paris. I have been there. Once. With a niece of mine. So what’s this ticket been left here for? The obvious reason, it would seem, is that some tourist returned from the Middle-East, now arrived in Paris, has left it in error. But the idea also enters the mind that the ticket has been left there in order to transmit a communication of some kind. What makes me think this, I can’t tell. But it doubtless has to do with the half-human half-animal creature illustrated in the centre of the ticket, and its associations with riddles, crime, incest. What the communication could therefore be, I can’t tell. And for whom it should be destined, I can’t tell either. I’m in the dark. I look around, in case I’ve taken a seat which was destined for another, but there are no obvious candidates. The likelihood that the communication was intended for me seems slim. I can think of no-one who is aware that I’m in Paris, nor can I think of a reason that would cause someone to communicate with me in this indirect fashion. What could the communication be in this case? It could be to advise me to travel to Karnac, but whatever for? And when? On the tenth? Le dix? It's difficult to work out. Just monomania. Let it lie. Yet I'd love a vacation in Karnac. I've wanted to return there for some time. See the relics once more, before I die. Think about the riddles. Which animal has four feet at dawn, two at noon and three at dusk? Man. Or the incestuous son himself. I've never had a desire to kill father. He was never alive in the true sense of the word to start with.

At the next table sits a customer who looks like Abraham Lincoln, or Bernard Shaw, without the beard. She mouths the words in silence as she reads from a fashion article in front of her on the table, which could be from *Elle* or *Marie Claire*. From time to time she takes a mouthful of Pastis, without so much as a look, or stretches her short tweed skirt down beneath her knees, where it remains for a moment, then rides back once more as she turns to the next feature. "Il a dit le contraire, c'est sure," intones someone behind me. "Picasso, c'est un connard," announces another. A Moroccan who sells trinkets from a small leather case comes over to me from the sidewalk and waves one of his best-sellers in front of me. "Dix francs," he announces. "C'est bon marché!" Attached to a small annulus is a diminutive rubber model of a baboon with a coloured bottom. "*Look!*" he announces. He takes it between his thumb and index and activates its hidden mechanism with a twist of his hand. At once, a massive red cock bursts out from between the baboon's truncated limbs. "C'est horrible," I announce. He flashes me a broad smile. "C'est bien naturel madame," he insists, then moves over to the next table. Without so much as a look in his direction, the woman who reads *Marie Claire* dismisses him with a wave of her hand. The barman comes back, tells him to "fichez les clients la solitude", then slams down a café crème and water, with the bill. It is at least three times as much as I had calculated for. I look into the recesses of the wallet I have with me, find all the small coins I can with which to settle the bill. Resolve n——

Krrreennnn! Krrreennnn! Jesus! *Krrreennnn!* What's this?! Someone has started to hammer at the door. *Krrreennnn! Krrreennnn!* Christ! It'll cave in if he carries on like that. OK, OK! I'm on the case! The warder shouts abuse at me, tells me to shift that fuckin'...oooff!...arse if I want some food to eat. I scramble over to the hatch, check to see if the blindfold's still on, that's fine, then shove the mess tin in. I hear him ladle the stew in, then he shoves it back. Like an automaton I crawl back to the bed where I lie, exhausted. I taste the thin, unwholesome stew which on this occasion, as on most other occasions, has a bland, saltless taste. It is lukewarm, as usual, a fact which has led me to infer that the warder must visit a lot of other cells before mine. It could be that this cell lies towards the end of an immense corridor, but if this is the case it is odd that I do not hear him hammer the cane on other doors before I hear it on this one. As usual I scoff the stew, bad as it is. I need to calm the wild animal which chews at the heart of the stomach. There'll be no more now till breakfast.

When I've finished the stew I feel the need to void the bowels. Blind, I crawl on all fours to where the bucket stands in the corner. I don't need to be able to see for this. Such is the stench I could sniff it out if I had to, like a bloodhound, or a blind mole. It stands in the corner that faces the sink, an emblem of filth which faces an emblem of cleanliness. I ease down the trousers, sit on the cold steel rim. The rusted metal sinks a bit under me as I relax with an exordial fart. Prrrrrrrfffff! Ridiculous as it will seem, I become embarrassed at times like this. In case the warder or one of his auxiliaries should hear me. Or whoever else lurks in the corridor, for that matter. But there's no need to. To fart is as natural as to breathe or to walk or to run, and commences before we are born. I'm sure the warder and his auxiliaries, and the Lieutenant, and even the Colonel, and even the little man that sits between them behind the wide desk fart as well, damn it. Most folk do. At a mean rate of twelve times in 24 hours, I've heard it said. And then the diet here doesn't do the intestines much of a favour, to be sure. So the warder and his chums have no reason to take me to task for the odd fart or two. Besides, it's no more than once or twice a visit. I shouldn't have mentioned it.

Beneath me I feel the warmth of the stewed excrement in the bottom of the bucket, and once more the smell invades the nostrils. A fricassee of fart and shit with a hint of rusted metal in urine. The warder doesn't seem over-anxious to clean it out, and who can blame him, it's a thankless task, but I wish he'd do so soon, before I'm sat in the stuff. *Ahhh!* That's better. *Schlooossshh!* Hear it fall. Tumble into the slime.

Yet what would I do if it started to leak over the rim? If the worst came to the worst I'd have to do it on the floor. I'd be reluctant, all the same. Even in these abominable conditions I like to maintain certain standards. Otherwise one lets them have a head start. In the end, too, it would trickle all over the floor. I'd be forced to crawl about in it, covered from head to toe. Yet have to hoist the neck clear of the shit, so as to breathe. The warder would have to come and clean it all out then. Unless the warder, the Colonel and the rest of them started to think I was on one of those shit strikes. Then I'd be chastised to boot. Marvellous! For two weeks one crawls about in shit, covered from head to toe in one's own excrement, for no fault of one's own, then one is clobbered for it, as if one had tried to rob a bank, or driven a car at 90 in a residential area. Quick. Better dash to the sink and wash these hands. That's another insult. No toilet roll. Unless it's the custom round here, who knows? The faucet rattles and shakes and a thin trickle of water comes out. Smells as if it's run over a number of hands like mine once before, more than once before indeed. Better than a rub off on the walls all the same. Be thankful for small mercies.

*

Tak...tak.

What on earth's that noise? I wish to God it's not the warder back. Tak...tak...tak. No. It's not from the door. What then? Need to locate it. Listen.

Tak...tak...tak. I think it comes from the wall that faces the bed. Quick. Crawl over and check it out. Perchance it's a break-out team, come to tunnel me out? Friends from back home who've heard about me! Taken it into their own hands! But who'd do that for me? How would one hear? One week I'm there, one week I'm not, who's the wiser? Folk would think I've decided not to answer calls, that's all. Not unlike me either. Used to do that sometimes. Or tear the wire out of the wall. The wall. Yes, it's from the wall, for sure, and now I'm a little closer I can tell it's not the noise of shovels. Tak...tak. There it is once more. Quiet, ordered, insistent, like morse code or the like. That's it! Someone wants to communicate with me! That's what it is. The inmate in the next cell? I knock on the wall with both fists to let them know I'm here, but all I achieve for this trouble is a hollow thunk. Quick. Get the mess tin. Knock with that.

Tak...tak...tak. That's her, on the other side of the wall. Or him. I send the ball back. Tak...tak. Two taks, so she doesn't think it's an echo. At once, there's a whole run of taks in answer.

Tak...tak...tak...tak...tak...tak...tak...tak.
Tak...tak...tak...tak...tak...tak...tak...tak...tak.

8, then 9. A communication, of some sort. Been there since 89? Could be. Or for 89 weeks? 8 and 9. Makes 17. Years lived on earth at time of arrest? Yet it could be letters, each number linked to a letter. 1=A, 2=B, 3=C, 4=D, and so on. 8 and 9, then, would be... A,B,C,D,E,F,G,H. A,B,C,D,E,F,G,H,I. H and I. H-I! A salutation! Bit familiar, but down-and-outs can't be choosers. Quick. Send it back. Alter it a bit so as to see it works.

Tak...tak...tak...tak...tak...tak...tak...tak.
Tak...tak...tak...tak...tak.
Tak...tak...tak...tak...tak...tak...tak...tak...tak...tak...tak ...tak.
Tak...tak...tak...tak...tak...tak...tak...tak...tak...tak...tak ...tak.
Tak...tak...tak...tak...tak...tak...tak...tak...tak...tak...tak ...tak...tak...tak...tak.

Christ! That took a while. Must be the reason she chose H and I. Live and learn, as it's often remarked. Listen.

Tak...tak...tak...tak...tak...tak...tak...tak...tak...tak...tak ...tak...tak...tak...tak.
Tak...tak...tak...tak...tak...tak...tak...tak...tak...tak...tak.

What's that? 15, 11. A,B,C,D,E,F,G,H,I,J,K,L,M,N,O. A,B,C,D,E,F,G,H,I,J,K. O and K. O-K! I send back the same. 15 taks, then 11. O-K! Now we're in business.

The taks start once more. 23, 8, 1, 20. Silence. 9, 19. Silence. 25, 15, 21, 18. Silence. 14, 1, 13, 5. End. What does that make? Let's see.

W-H-A-T-I-S-Y-O-U-R-N-A-M-E?

I tell them. Then ask the same. A man's name. Then he starts over.

H-O-W-A-R-E-Y-O-U?

I tell him. Ask the same. He taks out he's well, like I did, even if he's not, I'm not.

W-H-A-T-W-A-S-Y-O-U-R-O-F-F-E-N-C-E?

I tell him I don't know. Throw it back at him. He's in the same boat. Doesn't know. I ask him what he's been accused of. He tells me. Same as me. More or less. The one difference seems to be that the Colonel hasn't called me a homosexual, hasn't called him a whore. I ask him about other issues, or he asks me. Questions.

Place of birth. Job. Married or unmarried. Children. Favourite colour. As it turns out he used to run a kebab stall, 24/7. Must be how he can do all these taks at this hour. Before that he was an itinerant salesman. Toilet rolls, underwear, socks, bubble bath, and the like. Round Colchester and north-east Essex.

H-A-V-E-Y-O-U-A-N-Y-E-S-C-A-P-E-P-L-A-N-S?

That's what he asks next. Tell him no. What are his?

D-I-G-A-T-U-N-N-E-L.

I ask the obvious.

W-H-A-T-W-I-T-H?

He doesn't know. Asks me if I have an idea. I tell him no, unless we use our bare hands. He taks out he's tried it. Doesn't work. I'm tired with all these taks. Too much concentration. Tell him so. Finish off for now.

L-E-T-S-S-L-E-E-P-O-N-I-T.

He taks OK. Taks out a slow au revoir. I do likewise.

All those taks have done for me. Goes to one's head. Never known the interminable hours of darkness seem so short, but. It's been some session. Yet we'll have to tinker with that code a bit. Laborious, as it stands. Too arcane for sure. If I could remember the codes in that book father used to have. *Codes and Cribs*, that was it. Alexander D'Abakeleff. There were loads in there. Civil, martial, divine, all sorts. Illustrated as well. But all of them too elaborate to remember. Had to be, I take it. Otherwise too much of a doddle to crack. Don't fret, let it be for now. Snooze on it.

I could do with a calmative to send me off. A calmative. But I've scoffed all the bread. Christ. Hard to shut that endless tak-tak-tak out of one's head. Tak...tak ...tak! Tak...tak! I know. The lists. Writers. Do a more difficult one this time, that should do it, that should do it. Drift into the arms of Somnus. Novelists this time. A to Z. Let's see.

Austen
Balzac
Cervantes
Dickens
Eliot

Faulkner
Gaskell
Hesse
Isherwood

James

Kafka A net went in search of a bird.

Lawrence	
Mann	
Nabokov	
Orwell	???????
Pasternak	
Queneau	
Robbe-Grillet	
Sterne	No odd book will last.
Tournier	
???????	Can't think. Don't fret.
	Back on to that later.
Verne	*Around the World in...*
	three months was it?
	Wonder where I'll be in three months' time?
Uris!	
	Where would I like to be?

Got woken while it was still dark. He does that sometimes, for the sheer hell of it as far as I can see. One of their little tricks. He comes in with some ridiculous excuse or other. This time it was a routine search. Or so the warder said. Stormed in like a herd of cattle, four or five of them at once, lifted me out of bed and shoved me onto the wall arms akimbo. One of them carried a rifle with which he hit me in the back while the others continued with the search. The first concern, after the initial shock, when I feared one of them would shoot me, was for the recess. The warder hadn't closed the door behind him, so there was a fair chance he wouldn't notice it, but if he decided to close it for some reason or other then it would be a whole new kettle of fish. I had eaten the bread – I've said that, I think – but there were bound to be a few tell-tale crumbs, nonetheless. If there were there'd be sure to be another cross-examination afterwards. Whatever, there was little I could do about it now. The best I could do was not to sneak a look in the direction of the door, which wasn't difficult, not with a rifle in one's back, and the blindfold on.

After the warder and his cronies had scouted around the bed and rooted about the sink there wasn't much else to search, so the warder started to march around the cell and hammer on the walls with his truncheon. The others did likewise. I don't know what the visitors wanted to achieve with this. The warder could have been on the lookout for a tunnel, but I don't think so. For if he had been, he would, without doubt, have bent down on his hands and knees. One doesn't start to hollow out a tunnel six feet above the floor, at least not if it's to remain a secret, and I'm sure it was round about this mark, sometimes at an even more elevated level, that the warder hammered. There seemed to be little reason behind his actions, there was a slavish side to them, as if he himself had no real idea what he was about. It had become a mere routine for him, as it had for his cronies, and if it had once had a clear aim, he was now as unaware of what this could be as I was. For a moment I started to feel for him, but the moment did not last. The immediate concern was the friend in the next cell. If he were to hear them knock on the walls he could think I wanted to communicate. And if he started to tak now we'd both be done for. As chance would have it, he didn't. It was fortunate for me, as it was for him, that he was not so foolish as to mistake the noise of a search for the noise of a communication.

A few minutes later the warder left with the other visitors, and he seemed satisfied. If the intention of their visit had been to rob me of rest, it had been a success, no doubt about it. I sat down on the bed. Knees at 90°, elbows on knees, head between hands. It seemed to me that mere seconds had slid round the dial since the moment I'd rattled off the list of novelists to make me relax. Yet as I sat there, in the dark, the half-faded recollection of a dream started to form itself in the mind.

I had dreamt I was a mole, hundreds of feet under the earth. The earth was cold and wet, and it had a fetid smell, more that of excrement than soil. I wanted to burrow to the earth's surface, feel sun once more on skin and face. I aimed what had become a snout towards the heavens and started to burrow for all I was worth with these little mole-hands of mine. Tunneled for hours, on and on in the darkness. In the end I felt the earth become drier, more friable, less dense. A moment later, the snout broke out into the air. I was dazzled in a blaze of sunshine. No sooner had I surfaced, however, than a monstrous flat shovel crashed down on me; it drew blood, and made me scuttle off under the earth at once. A little later I tried to surface once more, a bit further on. Once more the shovel crashed down, and made me scuttle off under the earth as before. Cut an interminable tale short, each time I tried to surface the same shit kicked off. Soon as the snout broke out in the air, down came the shovel. A little while later the search must have woken me. At least I'd had time to dream, then. After the A-Z of authors. Before the warder came. But I don't think I can have rested as well as I'd have liked. Whatever, I felt exhausted. Still do, come to think of it.

Krrriinnnn! Krrriinnnn! Here's the warder with the breakfast. About time too. *Krrriinnnn!* Quick as I can I seize the mess tin, a bit dented from the unannounced visit, and shuffle over to the door. Once there, it's the usual routine. First locate the hatch. Then shove the mess tin into the hole. Hear him fill it. Then return it. First for the coffee, then the oats. Both cold, as usual. Bolt them down nevertheless, as usual. Feel a little sick now, but I don't think I'll vomit. Please to God not. But who can tell? Wish for the best and be in readiness for the worst, as I've heard said. It's the lack of rest, I think. Does that sometimes. Unless the warder's added some toxic element to the food. He does that, I'm sure of it. Another of their tricks. Better lie down all the same. Horizontal better than vertical. See if I can doze a little. Switch off.

*

Couldn't doze off. Tried, but no luck this time. Once bitten twice bashful, as is often said. Went over the list of hobbies.

Walks
Maxims
A-Z lists
Patois (invent own)
Inventories

Most attractive the maxims, worsen some I know from childhood. Like *You cannot have an ache and treat it* instead of *cake and eat it*. That sort of stuff. I was about to set to work on this, first with a brainstorm to collect some material to start with, when I hit on a better idea. I don't think I invented it, this idea. I think I must have seen it once in a TEFL textbook, or some such. Whatever, all of a sudden it struck me I could have a bash at it. The idea was to write a kind of fictional conversation between two bodies. It had to consist of 26 words, and each word had to start with a different letter, from A-Z. A first, Z last. It was a kind of vocab exercise, I think. Part of its attraction, at least for me, was that without ink or a notebook I would still be able to do it, the A-Z structure a kind of aide-mémoire. Whatever, I had a bash. I liked the result a lot. Nonsense, of course. If I can still remember it, it went more or less like this:

– A BRAZEN COW.

– DID EDGAR FINE.

– GOD!

– HIS IMPERIAL JEZEBEL, KILLED LAST MONDAY.

– NO OBITUARY.

– PICKAXED. QUEEN ROSE SOBBED.
– TINY UNDERTAKER'S VAN, WHAT?
– XENOPHOBIC YOUTH!
– ZEITGEIST.

Doesn't seem so brilliant now. And in terms of historical content it's inaccurate on several counts. But then, so what? The historical is the bad dream one does one's best to snooze off! It was fun at the time, whatever. That's what counts. And I can use it in future if I have to, if I run out of ideas. Both the formula and the text. Translate it into French. That would kill some time. Or German. But it would be difficult to maintain the A-Z backbone. Whatever, it's made the first shift start well. Thankful for small mercies.

*

The warder's been in to see me once more. I seem to be his favourite at the moment. Didn't invite his friends this time. Unlocked the door without so much as a knock and marched over to where I was stretched out on the bed. I had a decent look at him for once, for while I still had the blindfold on it was not as secure as usual, and I could see all I needed to via a little tear in the material. As I looked into his face as if to extract therefrom some sort of hidden rationale for his visit, his mouth broadened to form a toothless smile, then he took out a box of biscuits and threw them onto the bed. Without clarification he turned on his heels and headed for the door. He'd left it more or less shut, so that, as he went out, it wouldn't have been difficult for him to see the recess, had he been on the lookout for it. As it turned out he didn't, but he must have noticed the little white mark on the hole's cover. He came to a standstill, and rubbed it a little with his sleeve, but there was no indication that he had made a connection between what he saw and the activities of the inhabitant of the cell. He didn't rumble me, in a word. So much the better. If he did I'll learn about it sooner or later. But somehow I think he did not. Call it a hunch, as it's said in the movies. It could be he mistook it for bird shit, for all I know, but how on earth he thinks a bird flew in here, I can't tell.

Now that I think of it, I've heard their tune at times, but where it comes from I can't be sure. It could be that there's a tree on the other side of the little window in the roof. Who knows? Whatever the case, there sure as damn it aren't birds in the cell. Not now, for certain. But it could be there have been, in former times. Perchance, before I came here, the warder unlocked the little window in the roof, to air the cell a bit between inmates, and in flew a little bird. A blackbird, for instance. Or a thrush. Or the bird that caused Tereus's wrath in Ovid's tale. Philomel! The warder befriended it. Gave it a name. Came in to see it each dawn. Held out in his coarse hands the little sunflower seeds he'd collected for it. Then one time he came to find the bird had flown. All in a flash, then, this little scenario runs into his mind, as he rubs the little blob of dentifrice, which he mistakes for bird shit, off the hole.

One's conscience starts to tell one it's unfair, to deceive him like this. But not for more than a moment. In all likelihood there had never been a bird, nor, indeed, did there have to have been to understand the warder's actions. He sees a blob. He removes it. In a word, I don't think the warder was all that clever. At least he didn't seem to be. For sure, he was not a fantastic communicator, and seemed to be of a rather lone and mole-like cast of mind. Whether he had forever been so, or had become like that over the decades as he walked these sinuous corridors and into these cold, dark cells, it is hard to tell.

I sit on the bed and count the biscuits, set them out in stacks of 6. There are sufficient biscuits for 6 stacks and 2 left over, which I eat at once. That leaves 6 stacks of 6 biscuits, 36 biscuits in all. Sufficient for 12 over 24 hours for 3 lots of 24 hours, or, if I take it slow, 6 in 24 hours for 6 lots of 24 hours. If one takes a theoretical view, of course, I could make them last almost forever, for 36 lots of 24 hours, for instance, at 1 biscuit in 24 hours. Or for an even more extended time still, if I broke them into bits. But if I went to such extremes I know the little self-control I have would crack, and that the method, like the biscuits, would fall to bits. No, it would be far more sensible to stick to 12 in 24 hours for 3 lots of 24 hours and have done with it. Be realistic. At least like that one won't let oneself down. And it's essential not to let oneself down at times like these. To create a method, however basic, and stick to it is a terrific boon. In difficult times. And even in times not as adverse as all that, it does no harm. That's what I think, for what it's worth. 12 in 24 hours, then. For three lots of 24 hours.

At once I devour 6 of them, and am still famished. So I devour 6 more. After 12 the esurience is still not abated. The diet here is so minimal that even if I devoured all 36 it would not make much difference, but it would make me sick, for certain. Whatever, I leave off after 12, cautious as I am not to subvert the method. Anal, one could think. No, rather banal. The kind of banal that is forced on one of limited means. Whatever, I reckon that the broth will be delivered soon with its ration of bread, and it would be wise to leave room for it.

Just as I reach this conclusion, I detect a little hole in one of the back teeth as I lick around the mouth for biscuit crumbs. There has never been reason to write home about these teeth of mine, durableness is not one of their characteristics, and this sudden and excessive feast of biscuits after a diet of oats, broth and stew must have been too much for them. The hole, however, is on the small side, and on further examination the rest of the tooth seems to be more or less sound. It has been filled once before, I had the deed done in Exmouth, Devon, ill done, as deeds tend to be done there, and the hole is a result of a bit of metal fill-in which has fallen out near the centre. While the remains of the fill-in rest intact, however, I shouldn't have too much trouble. Not for a while, touch wood. If I ease off the biscuits. The broth, at least, shouldn't be too difficult. Nor the bread, but it would be wise to dunk it. I'll do that. It will make a nice variation. Remind me of old times.

*

I was sat in the cell and looked forward to the arrival of the broth, when the warder and his cronies came to fetch me. All of them this time. Can't seem to leave me alone for once. And it's said *absence* makes the heart become fonder! Some mischief's afoot, I can tell. But it's all chaff to the mill as far as I'm concerned. I could tell where the warder would take me, and this time I was mindful to follow the route in the mind, or at least do the best I could. I think we went left out of the cell door then walked for some distance down what must be the external corridor. I can't be sure, for all the time the warders manhandled me, one on either side clutched me under the arms, and another followed close behind, who shoved me if I didn't make sufficient haste, but I had a sense that the corridor curved a little, to the left, as if we walked but a small section of what was in truth a far vaster arc. After a bit we turned off, to the left, and descended several stairs. I lost track of matters a little after that, but there were more stairs for sure and more corridors before we arrived at the cross-examination room. The warder took off the blindfold as soon as I was inside. The little man was there behind the wide table. He's the Governor, I must've said that. So was the Colonel. The Lieutenant's chair, this time, was untaken. Could it be he was on annual leave? Perchance, at that exact moment, he strode towards some devilish bunker, with his caddie close behind, in chase of his sliced tee shot? The little man – the Governor, that is – smiled and asked me if I had received the biscuits. I said I had. He disclosed that, unfortunate as it was, I would have to miss the broth. That he had not been able to fit me in at another time. Added that he believed that detainees should be well fed nonetheless, so had sent the biscuits. I didn't thank him. I didn't intend to thank someone when I was fobbed off with a lunchtime slot.

He asked how I found the cell. Said he was concerned. The Colonel nodded. I didn't believe them. How did I fill the time? What did I do in the afternoons? How did I find the view? I said I was well and found it rather comfortable. Told them I was at work on a thesis on the behavioural habits of moles. Moles? said the Colonel. Whatever for? Because I live in darkness like the moles, I said. It was a sentence from Petőfi, the writer, I don't think the Governor would have heard of him. Cross-examiners and modern verse don't on the whole intersect, at least it's not the norm, even if one remembers the Nazis' fondness for Goethe. I was rather taken with this little retort, but I don't think the Governor could have been. He wanted me to moan about the conditions. I was sure, moreover, that the biscuits were a direct hint from him that he was able to treat me in a much better manner, if I'd collaborate. If I did so, I could have a better room, illumination, a chair, and on the whole more access to the kind of luxuries we take in our stride in normal life. Exercise, clean clothes, a bath, a ticket to the cinema, a candlelit dinner, a taxi, a bottle of wine, a toothbrush. That was what the biscuits seemed to mouth. At least to me. If biscuits can be said to seem to mouth.

The Colonel stood at this moment and looked at me with a stern stare. What's the use of this resistance? he asked. You will be broken, like all the others. We've broken harder nuts than this, he said to the Governor. I didn't answer. Just stared at the wall in front of me without so much as a flinch. He must have believed that the best contrivance at that moment was to let me alone in the cell for a while, alone with the biscuits. Let the biscuits talk. Whatever the truth of it, that's where the cross-examination came to an end. I wasn't hit on this occasion. The Colonel and the Governor must have tried to show me their nice side. But I could see their little trick a mile off, I could read them like a book, and was more determined than ever not to collaborate with them. I still like tennis now and then, and boules too, not to mention badminton, and there was an element of tennis, of boules, of badminton in all this. I knew there was no chance that I would win, the odds were stacked in their favour, but at least I could hold them to a tie.

Back in the cell I lie on the bed and doze for a while. The warder wakes me as he hammers on the door with the stew. *Krrriinnnn! Krrriinnnn!* I let him hammer and shout abuse while I crawl over to the door with the mess tin, locate the hatch, then shove it in. He shoves it back, with a bit of bread this time, which I am over the moon about. A touch of kindness! Thankful for small mercies. I knew he had a soft side. He must have saved it from the broth. Must have noticed that I wasn't back in the cell at lunch and realised I'd need it later on. Could well have wandered about with it in his trousers all afternoon. Maintained its warmth for me. This seems the most credible scenario, to be sure. But I don't thank him for it. Don't want to be indebted to him. It's hazardous to be indebted to one's warders. Like with the biscuits. That's another of their little tricks. Because these cross-examiners are the sole human contact one has one starts to connect with them, and then one can start to collaborate, to humour them. Need to be careful on that score. Maintain a distance. Besides, I can't tell if the warder held on to this bread with me in mind. And there's no reason to let him have the benefit of the doubt. I can't even be sure that he knows who I am, let's face it, let alone that he harbours affections for me. There could have been an excess of bread this afternoon for reasons I'll never understand, so that he has to dole it out free to all of us, as he does when the broth comes round. Or it could be we've been handed tomorrow's bread this afternoon, to break the routine, and tomorrow there'll be no bread at lunchtime, but broth alone?

With this in mind I decide to save the bread, and stash it with care in the recess. Even if I have missed the broth I'm less ravenous than usual at this hour. No doubt because of the biscuits. But I think I could be off food for some reason or other. For sure, I've felt better. The fact is, for better or worse, one becomes used to the diet in here, and when it's altered one's stomach is in trouble at once, one's stomach is in the shit in the literal sense. Whatever, I swallow the stew. Otherwise it would become cold. Colder.

Talk of the devil! As soon as I finished the stew I felt sick. It was a stroke of fortune that I made it to the bucket before I honked. Smell of shit and vomit in the corner now. Hear the flies buzz round it. Trust I don't have to run back over there for a while. The mere idea of it makes one want to heave. I wonder if he did meddle with the food. If so, it must have been in the biscuits. Otherwise, if it had been in the oats, for instance, or the broth, or even the stew, all the internees would have been ill at once. Just think of it! Yet on reflection I don't think that would bother them all that much. In fact, the bastards would no doubt find the idea had its attractions. Kill several birds with one stone. Whatever, I blame the biscuits. Shame to throw them out, however. Leave it. For the moment. See how I feel after a snooze. It could be exhaustion alone. After all, it's been a hectic afternoon, not to mention the dawn raid. And in that case, the biscuits could come in useful.

*

The man in the next cell starts to tak.

H-E-L-L-O!

Quick as I can, I snatch the mess tin and crawl over to the wall. Tak back.

H-E-L-L-O!

His turn.

H-O-W-A-R-E-Y-O-U?

Me.

N-O-T-V-E-R-Y-W-E-L-L.

He asks me what the matter is, and I tell him I've vomited. I don't tell him about the biscuits. Too convoluted. Besides, he could become envious.

I-C-H-U-N-D-E-R-A-L-L-T-H-E-T-I-M-E.

That's what he taks next, chunder. Must be his word for vomit. Prison dialect no doubt. Have to remember that, chunder. Then he's off once more.

M-O-R-E-O-F-T-E-N-T-H-A-T-E-N-D-T-H-A-N-T-H-E-O-T-H-E-R.

That's what he taks. Then adds.

T-H-E-S-E-D-A-Y-S.

As clarification. Need to become accustomed to it, it would seem. Bite the bullet. Chunder. Nice word that. Hot little bites, hot little bite-sized bullets, afloat in bile. Chunder broth. *Have ee ad aar chunder terdee then Edith? Who's a clever un then?* Talked like that in that rest home I was in down in Devon that time. What's that he's said?

A-N-Y-I-D-E-A-S-O-N-D-I-G-G-I-N-G?

I tell him no. Then I tell him about the new ideas I've had on the code. I'd had the idea moments before he started to tak. Perchance I've mentioned it. Whatever, the idea was rather modest. It was no more than an idea, but a solid one. Effective. It was this.

As it stood, if we wanted to articulate the letter P, for

instance, we had to tak 16 times. And if we wanted to voice P-U-T-T-Y, for instance, we had to tak a total of 102 times. Yet if we had a shorthand means to indicate 10 taks, such as 2 taks in succession, or a double-tak, and a shorthand means to indicate 5 taks, such as 3 taks in succession, or a tri-tak, then it would be much easier to articulate the letter P. All we would need to do would be to make a double-tak, a tri-tak, and a standard tak and the business would be done. With this method, the letter P, if we counted double-taks as 2, and tri-taks as 3, even if this was not true, for double-taks were less than 2, and tri-taks were less than 3, could be articulated in a total of 6 taks instead of 16. And the word P-U-T-T-Y could be articulated in 26 taks and not 102. A reduction of 10 taks in the first instance and 76 in the second. Not inconsiderable, I reasoned.

The elucidation took some time, for the method it described had still to be instituted. When I had finished I asked him.

W-H-A-T-D-O -Y-O-U-T-H-I-N-K?

I used the new code for the first time. 70 taks instead of 194. A reduction of 124 taks. I was sure he'd be excited. Listened out for his answer.

N-O-T-B-A-D, he said.

He could have been a bit more enthusiastic, but at

least he used the revised code. Must have his reservations about new methods. It's almost certain he's been here for a more extended time than I have. Doesn't like innovation. Still, it's his fault, for he made the first contact. He's made his bed. I told him that it would enable us to communicate more in less time, and that therefore there would be less chance of detection. He concurred, but I had the sense he resented this innovation of the old code. For sure, he had become more than a tad silent all of a sudden. Then it occurred to me that it could be that he didn't have much to discuss, or that he even harboured some hidden secret. Some skeleton in his closet, some stiff buried at the bottom of his orchard, some madwoman in his attic.

I draw our business to a close.

L-E-T-S-L-E-A-V-E-I-T-T-H-E-R-E-F-O-R-N-O-W-I-M-S-L-E-E-P-Y.

He taks back.

O-K.

Then we tak our shortened farewells.

G-O-O-D-N-I-G-H-T!

N-I-G-H-T!

In the hours of darkness I had another dream. Not to do with moles this time. I was in a hotel room. A tall brass bed stood next to one of the walls. There was a French window, which overlooked trees and an estate. There was a writer's desk in one corner, I remember, with lots of little drawers in the columns, and a leather veneer. In the corner there was a little sink unit with a bidet beside it. A door stood between this room and the one next door. From behind it I could hear a faint moan, as if someone needed aid but had lost all belief that it would come. While I had no idea who the resident could be, I felt I had to enter and offer them succour. I tried the door, which was unlocked, and strode into the room. The shutters had been closed and it was dark and airless. Yet after a few moments I could see that almost the entire room was filled with a funereal bed as wide as it was tall. Its curtains were drawn, and a thin little old woman rested in it with the white sheet tucked under her chin. Her face was emaciated, her faded hair fell to the floor in knots. Her arms, which were motionless outside the blankets, were withered like sticks. It was clear at once that she was about to die. Yet somehow I felt I had to wake her, as if there were some secret force that drove me on. I started to shake her, but there was no answer. So I shook her in a still more forceful manner. Still, no answer. As she continued to resist these efforts, so the need to wake her became more acute. More and more, I felt that if I could elicit from her some kind of answer, however small, somehow, like a miracle worker, I could resurrect her from the dead, and, moreover, not her life alone, but mine too, somehow rested on this. Frantic, I started to shout at her. *Awake! Awake!* I hit her about the face. *Awake, in God's name, woman!* I hit her over and over and over, in a kind of mad trance, and I continued to shout at her as I did so. When I was about to cease for want of success there was at last a small flicker of movement. Her head, which a moment before had lain flat on the bolster, lifted towards me, and she looked at me out of her small round irises. Looked me in the face.

Odd moments occur in dreams. Their stories follow laws we don't understand, and their sudden shifts of location and view show little concern for our sense of the rational. Moreover, and witnesses bear this out, dreams are more visual than verbal, so that when we translate them into words we often iron out their oddities in our need to rationalise them. On another occasion I would have said that this dream ended here, or that its end was blurred, and that later I had another dream, more shattered, in which the Colonel and the Lieutenant cross-examined me. But I feel sure that that was not the case. That the two were in fact one.

Perchance it could be stated a little clearer. Perchance I make a mountain out of a molehill, I don't know. In either case, what occurred next I remember like this. At the exact moment the woman unclosed her lids and looked me in the face, all of a sudden I wasn't there. Or rather, when she unclosed her lids and looked at me, as I stood over her, it was not her visual cortex that transmitted the data, but mine, and I did not look down at her, but looked towards the roof, from inside her head.

The Colonel stood before me, and looked down. He smiled, and moved back a little. Then he held a massive cracked mirror in front of me. Take a look, he said. You are old and weak and have little will left. You are a fool to resist. We have cracked harder nuts than this! I looked in the cracked mirror which he continued to hold before me as if to demonstrate the truth of what he said. The retinal area was blue and hollow, the face wizened like an old walnut, the hair fell in lank and knotted locks to the floor. The arms stuck out of their sockets like sticks. It was clear that I was about to die.

It was a horrible dream, and it woke me with a start. I was cheerful about this, after the initial shock, for I did not want it to continue. It's a kind of defence mechanism, I think, one wakes at the worst moment. I've even heard it said that if one dreams one's death, falls off a cliff, for instance, and hits the beach below, one kicks the bucket for real. But it doesn't occur often. Most often one wakes as one starts to fall. Just feels the shock. But then how can one tell in such a case? Hotline to God in heaven? Seances with dead dreamers? I'd taken a little snooze in the front room when all of a sudden I must have dozed off and started to dream I was in the car when all of a sudden the car hit another car and then all of a sudden I was here above or down below well it's difficult to tell in actual fact but it's not bad all the same. Over and out. Could be it's done with tests on animals. Rats, mice, rabbits. That sort of creature. But then what would a rabbit want to dream itself to death for? It's not as if there were an afterlife for them, is it? Curious.

*

I had an interminable wait till breakfast. When it came, I was in wait. The warder can't have known what had hit him. I was sat beside the door, mess tin in hand, and almost as soon as his cane struck I lifted the hatch as best I could from the inside and shoved the mess tin in. He must have heard the noise of the hatch as it clicked, and he could even have seen the mess tin as it materialised on cue for once from the other side of the door, but it all occurred with such haste that he hammered the cane on the door once more nonetheless, even if its work was done. *Krrroonnnn!* He huffed, then he filled the mess tin with coffee. Pushed it back. I swallowed it down, for I was ravenous, then shoved it back for the oats. When it came back, the oats were cold, as usual. Yet for once I felt a bit let down, for the utmost effort had been made to act with due haste and thus allow the oats a fair chance to remain hot. And all in vain. If I'm not mistaken, the oats were even colder than usual. But what could I do? I ate a few mouthfuls, but it was too much. I was ravenous, but it was clear, this time, I was not as ravenous as all that. I threw the oats into the bucket. *Schluuuck!*

Almost at once I mourn the rash loss of the oats. It's a fair wait till lunch and even now the stomach's started to rumble. It must be even hollower than usual, what with that chunder. That's the word, isn't it? Better ask the man later. If I can remember. I could do with a nice walk about the cell. That should calm the old stomach down. Jesus. It's started to creak like a coffin-lid! I'll have to invent some contrivance. Take the mind off it, at least. If I could take the blindfold off it would be nice. Have a root around the cell. See if there's some stuff I've not noticed before. I could shift it about a bit, for sure. The blindfold. So that I can see out of a little tear in the material. But then there's still the brain-teaser of the door. The hole.

I know! It's a bit of a risk. But let's do it. What is there to lose? Quick, off with the blindfold. I crawl over to the hole, silent as I can, to see if I can shift it from the inside. If the warder looks in now I'll be done for. Let's see. Yes. No trouble there. I take a look. Blank. Good. I fetch the dentifrice, with all the haste I can muster, smear a small blob on the side of the hole cover. Close it. Good. He won't be able to rumble this. When he slides it aside I'll see the dentifrice stuck to the side, know that I'm watched. When he closes it I won't, I'll know that I'm safe. And he never fails to close it before he comes in. So won't see it, won't mistake it for bird shit. There. Can't fail.

Should be safe now. Just double-check. Yes. Can't see the dentifrice, must be OK in that case. Let's have a look round then. Don't rush. But remember to have a look at the hole now and then. I take stock of the bed, the sink, the foldable table, the bucket. All in order in the dim. I look once more at the cracks, which start in the centre of the room, then broaden as their tentacles reach the walls where, here and there, the cracks are stuffed with bits of old broadsheets, cloth, and sacks. Head tilted, I look at the small black window in the roof, its second-hand luminescence as it falls down. I rub cheeks and face over the walls, smell the wet, the mould. There isn't much else.

But wait. I don't see it, but there is a noise I'm not familiar with. Like the rustle of leaves, the scratch of a nib as it moves across a notebook, or the scuttle of a beetle. Or a mouse. A rat. I take the mess tin, the sole means of defence, in case it's ferocious. Follow the noise. There. Over towards the sink. Quick. It's ended now. Sit still. Wait. Minutes tick. Not a sound. More minutes tick. Then there it is once more. All of a sudden I see a little dormouse, beneath where I'm crouched. It rests on its hind feet, nose in the air, its two black beads shine in the darkness. Unaware of me, it nibbles at what must be an ear of corn, unless I'm mistaken. Where it found an ear of corn in here it's hard to think. Must have carried it in from the outside. So there must be an exit then, for a mouse, at least. Merciless, I slam the mess tin down on it. *Klok!* Got it. I slide a hand underneath, turn it over. Peer in. The dormouse looks at me with a stare that seems to accuse. I turn it out into the hand. Put down the tin. I stroke it. Talk to it. It's OK, I tell it. We can be friends. Ask it daft details. Where is its home? Where are its little friends? What is its business here? It runs via the left arm, across the left shoulder, behind the neck, across the other shoulder, down the other arm and into the other hand. I hold it between enclosed hands. Place it in the sink to be safe. It tries to run over the sides, but small as the sink is it slithers back before it has climbed far. I leave it there. The little dormouse. Feel content that I have a friend at last. I could learn to communicate with it, Like Saint Francis with the birds, like Doctor Doolittle. Teach it to talk. Or learn to talk to it. Whatever, it's nice to feel another live creature, however small. And to have some contact with the outside world, however tentative.

*

Krrroonnnn! Krrroonnnn! That'll be the warder back. So soon! With the broth and bread. Quick as I can, I slide the blindfold back on, seize the mess tin and hobble over to the door. I'm used to it now. Could do it while I snoozed. I shove the mess tin into the hole. He lifts it, ladles the broth in. This is the best moment. When one hears it but has still to taste it. He hands it back and I take hold of it, like a hound. Famished. Then he shoves the bread in, which I leave on the shelf. Quick as I can I swallow down the broth. Usual lettuce and water mixture. Rather bland this afternoon. When I've finished I'm still ravenous. Tuck into the bread at once, careful not to touch the tooth. Afterwards I need a drink. Take the mess tin to the faucet, fill it, careful not to harm the dormouse. Drink it down. It is stale and dirt-filled but satisfies one's thirst. Leaves a vile taste in the mouth all the same. If I'd been more alert I'd have reserved a little bit of bread till after, to rid the mouth of the taste. Too bad. You win some and lose some. Then I remember the dentifrice. Do it with some of that.

Now the endless hours of the afternoon stretch before me. With what shall I fill them? An afternoon walk, to start with, then followed with a little snooze. With luck, no more dreams. Where shall I walk, then? Rome? Berlin? Amsterdam? Yes, what's not to like about Amsterdam? Where should I start? That hotel I was in once, with the flowers in the windows, which overlooked the canal. Herentracht, was it? OK. Wander.

I leave the hotel on Herentracht that faces the stern edifice of the Bible Museum, which houses its collection of sacred texts and icons, and take a turn which leads me off from the buzz and confusion of the centre, its loud retail arcades, cafés and sex stores, which attract the crowds like children who have never seen sweets before. It is a warm, sunlit afternoon and the street is almost deserted, save for the occasional lost tourist and the odd woman on a bike. As I cross the street to be on the canalside, one of them almost knocks me down, she shouts abuse at me in Dutch, words I don't understand. The cobbles here are uneven and narrow on the track for walkers. Between this and the road stand a row of cast-iron bollards, black in colour, fixed at intervals of around 6 feet. The canalside border, which falls off before it sinks beneath the surface of the water, is lined with a thick steel chain, which is attached to concrete abutments, which stand at even intervals of about 5 feet. At the summit of each abutment a steel annulet extrudes from the concrete, into which the chain is fixed. At the start of the street the 1st bollard and the 1st abutment are fixed so as to face each other. As one walks on, however, the distance between them increases: each successive bollard advances 1 foot on its nearest abutment, until, at the 6th bollard and the 7th abutment, the two once more fall into line. Thus, for each 7 abutments I count on the left, I count a mere 6 bollards on the other side, as I advance down Herentracht.

The canal water is dark and unwholesome, and in its surface one can see reflections of trees and of the tall narrow merchants' houses which stand on the other bank. From time to time a boat is seen, and in the wash it leaves behind it the reflections scatter into a thousand bits, which, one at a time, coalesce once more to reveal, a little further on, reflections of different trees, different tall narrow houses. As I draw near a stone arch that crosses the water, I see beneath it the rusted bonnet of an old car which sticks out at 45° from the water. The vehicle's immatriculation number is half-visible beneath the broken radiator, but it too shows tokens of corrosion and most of the enamelwork has come off, so that it is difficult to make out the number. Alone, the letter M can be made out, on the far left of the immatriculation number. The bollards here continue to stud the narrow track for walkers on the street side, at intervals of 6 feet, and seem to be intact, so it can be inferred that the car was driven between two of them. The concrete abutments and their steel chain are also intact here. But this is not to be wondered at. The abutments seem to be of recent date when considered in the context of the vehicle, which has rusted all over, and which, while nine-tenths underwater, reveals a model which is now out of fashion.

As I reach another arch that crosses the water on the left, I turn and cross it, and as I do so I tread over the rusted wreck of the old car, then advance down Harlenstraat. The street derives its name from a certain Doctor Van Harlen who had a famous dental concern here in the 1790s. Now, the sole reminder of this is the smaller and more modest dental concern in the same street in the hands of the Van Veldes, whose next-door window cabinet boasts an elaborate collection of dental kitsch, at the centre of which is an enormous model ferris-wheel constructed out of toothbrushes. Just after this I reach another canal, Keirstracht. It too is lined with trees and houses which can be seen reflected in the dark water. As a boat arrives, their reflections scatter in the wash that follows, then reform after the boat has vanished. I continue in the same direction, cross another stone arch, and walk down a narrow street flanked with cafés and restaurants, but which also contains a number of disused and rundown houses with boarded windows. Like those which line the canal, these are tall and narrow. Near the summit of each of their tiled roofs a steel bar sticks out, on the horizontal, at the end of which is attached a miniature wheel, around which a chain or a thick cord could be attached. In the door of one of these, a man in his twenties with a thick beard and discoloured teeth sits cross-limbed on the cobbles, as he molests the tourists attracted to the cafés with alternate demands for cash and offers of hashish. Now and then he articulates a sentence in the idiolect that is common with tourists, but most of what he announces is in Dutch, which I do not understand. While I am able to order a coffee, a snack, a beaker of wine or a meal, the Dutch I have is limited in the extreme. But this does not bother me on the whole, so talented are the Dutch at other idiolects. I cross another stone arch and take a turn down Prinsentracht. As I look across the canal I see the Westerkerk, where Rembrandt is buried. A little further on, on the same bank, Anne Frank's house, outside of which an endless line of tourists stretches down the street, as each awaits their turn to crowd into the small, bare room where for a time Anne Frank wrote her famous words before the Nazis arrested her and the rest of the household, before exile to Auschwitz.

After a while I cross to the other side of the road, where I am attracted to the window of a store that stands on the corner. In the window are frisbees, Indian masks, ice-skates, Chinese kites, marbles of all colours and sizes, and a number of small and beautiful handmade models: a clown, a banker, a milkman, a tattoo artist, a lion, a soldier, a doctor, a nurse, a robber, a rozzer. The rozzer is round and fat with a red face and blown out cheeks. He is dressed in blue, and wears the hard black hat characteristic of a British constable. The models all have oversized smokes inserted into their mouths.

I leave the store window and walk down Prinsentracht, cross another arch on one side and another canal on the other. A crowd of American tourists, who wear luminous red tracksuits with I'VE DONE EUROPE WITH EURODIP emblazoned on the back in white, crowd the sidewalk. "Gee, where's the Eiffel Tower?" asks one. "Can I use dollars here?" asks another. Soon after the canal, I turn off down Tuinstraat, which leads into the heart of the old Joordan district with its time-worn cafés, bars, restaurants, small stores and exhibition rooms. Its successive names – Jourdelain, Jaardoon, Jardan – are all deformations of Le Jardin, which dates from the time when this was the French district of the town. Most of the canals and sidewalks here have the names of flowers and shrubs. Laurierstraat, Rozenstraat, Bloemstraat.

I advance down Tuinstraat until I reach a wooden-fronted bar where I come to a halt and walk inside. I walk to the back where there is a free table in the far left-hand corner and take a seat. Various old-fashioned enamel advertisements for beer, coffee, tea and cake cover the walls. One of them, on the wall which faces where I sit, announces **VAN NELLE VOOR KOFFIE EN THEE** in bold black letters on blue enamel. Beneath the advertisement, at a table on his own, sits a man in a flat black hat who smokes a meerschaum. He reads a novel, but from here it is difficult to make out the title, both because of the distance and as a result of the manner in which he holds it, leant at 45° on the border of the table. I can make out no more than the letters CAPT— on the bottom left of the cover. The waiter arrives and I order a coffee in Dutch. He smiles, then adds, as he abandons Dutch himself, that I have excellent Dutch, then turns, and shouts the order across the bar before he vanishes into a recess where he takes further orders, or collects some tumblers, or sits down for a smoke. It is no doubt an ideal moment for him to do so for the bar is far from full, as it is that moment of the afternoon when it is too late for lunch but still too soon for a cake. Besides me and the meerschaum-smoker, no other clients are visible from where I sit, save for a fat woman in black at the bar, and two lovers in their twenties who've taken a window seat. The woman at the bar chain smokes, and from time to time looks at her watch in an irritated manner, which leads me to think that she awaits a friend, or an admirer, who is a little late. The lovers who sit in the window have finished their drinks some time since, and lean in a concentrated manner over a chessboard. Behind the man, who sits on the left, a handcrafted bulb with an enormous and multi-coloured artdeco shade is nailed to an overhead beam. In the window, in silver letters, an advertisement reads:

It advertises Amsterdam's most famous brand of beer, brewed from the water of the river Amstel, around which Amsterdam was founded in the C13th, after the channels of the river were dammed, and a series of dikes built, which released the surround——

*

The warder has been in once more. The bastard. It's obvious that he was on watch outside the cell. It was a stroke of luck that I had the blindfold on. Must remember to watch the hole now I've worked out a method. Must have become a little too involved, as I acted out the walk in the cell. Still, could have been worse. He didn't hit me. Just told me to cease all movement for the foreseeable future. Told me to lie on the bed. Said I looked as if I could do with some rest. He could be correct, too. Those mental walks tire me out. More so than a real walk would, and all the more so when one knows the town as a mere visitor. Paris was easier, I know it so much better. But then the less familiar has its own rewards. It's see-saws and round-abouts, as is often said. Better relax now. Lie back. Remember how that P.E. teacher used to do it. Start with the toes. That's it. Now the limbs. That's it. Now the thorax. The arms. The hands. Good. And now the head. Last but not least. Relax!

It's no use. Like self-mesmerism. Never works well. Need another there. Another sentient creature. I have the mouse, of course, but he wouldn't be much use. Beads too small. Need to be wider. Like those of that snake Kaa. What was that book called? Can't remember. No worries. What shall I do now, then? To kill time. Till tea. Could make another list of writers. Poets, for instance. Or list all the facts I know about some curriculum area or other. I know that's how that character in Tolstoi did it. Still can't remember the name of the tale. But make a list of what? I could inventorise characters in novels, for instance. Or see what birds I can name. Could do the same on all sorts of items. Trees, flowers, canines, cars, cheeses, wine even. Bordeaux, Chablis, Côtes du Rhône, Côtes de Duras, Entre-deux-Mers, Pommerol, and so on. Problem is the choice is so vast it's difficult to know where to start. And if one makes the list in A-Z order – and unless one does this I don't see how one can remember where one has reached, at least if one works without notebook and ink, as I do – then how does one know when to abandon a certain letter and advance to the next one? That's one reason to stick to one item for each letter, as I did with the writers. Like that, the whole endeavour becomes a little more focused, at least. Whatever, I'm not in the mood to make a list at the moment. The whole idea strikes me as tedious and trivial, to tell the truth. Like when one writes a list before one visits the food store. Better save it till some other time. When I'm more in the mood. To be frank, I'm a little tired now. The warder was correct.

*

I must have dozed off. The warder woke me when he came in with the stew. Bolted it down, as usual. Still famished. As usual. It struck me I could make more of the new trick with the dentifrice. So I took the blindfold off and found I was able to look round the cell at leisure. I lifted out some of the crushed broadsheets from the cracks near the base of the walls, and discovered that some of the news items and features could still be read, with a little effort. I envisioned that I would start to unfold each of the items in turn and flatten them out, then sort them as to content so as to construct a little archive for me to read. As I started to think like this, all of a sudden I noticed an odd fact, which was this. That while I had eaten the teatime stew a short time back, the faint illumination that fell from the little window in the roof, which I would have assumed would become fainter and fainter as the dusk drew in, and as the hours when the sun shines are subsumed with the hours of darkness, had started to become more and more luminous all the time. Which was remarkable. At first I reasoned that I must be mistaken, that the sensation must be the result of some kind of hallucination, for I knew that such states were not uncommon in those detained in isolated confinement. Yet as the moments wore on, I became more and more convinced that this was no hallucination, but that I had in fact witnessed a bizarre luminescent fluctuation. It occurred to me that as dusk drew in, the officials could be under orders to activate additional forms of illumination and suchlike, so that while it became dark this could create the illusion, at least from the cell, that it had become less dark. If that makes sense. But even via the darkened window I could tell that the increase in luminescence outside did not come from an artificial source. The sole alternative thesis I could think of was that the sun, as it sank, all of a sudden became more luminescent due to some kind of reflection on the horizon, over water for instance, before it sank at last, and that what I witnessed was such an event. For sure, I have read accounts of similar occurrences in the notebooks of sailors. But then I was not at sea. Not in the literal sense. Then it was that I heard the twitter of birds. And that what had been so obvious all the time struck me like a thunderbolt.

What I witnessed was the start of the dawn. And what I had eaten but now had not been stew at all, but oats. In other words, what I had all the time taken to be the dusk was not the dusk at all, but the dawn. And as when I had believed I eat stew for tea, and in truth eat oats for breakfast, so when I had believed I eat oats for breakfast, with weak coffee, I must in truth have eaten stew, with weak coffee, and this at lunchtime. Or it could be that what I had taken for coffee was in actual fact tea, for I reasoned that if I could mistake stew for oats, and oats for stew, I could with similar ease mistake tea for coffee. Indeed, I had remarked more than once that what I had all the time taken for coffee bore scant resemblance to what I had been served as such in the outside world, even in the most dubious of establishments. So it was the broth which I ate at dusk, then, with the side dish of bread, whereas till now I had taken this for the lunch.

Each stretch of 24 hours, therefore, did not start with oats and coffee, or oats and tea, to be followed at lunchtime with broth and bread, then at dusk with stew. But rather started with oats alone, with stew and coffee to follow, or stew and tea, and was concluded at dusk with broth and bread. It followed, therefore, that what I had assumed to be the hours of darkness, when I had endeavored to snooze, had in actual fact been the time that followed the dawn, for I had dozed after I ate the oats, which I had mistaken for the stew which I believed arrived at dusk. And when I had believed it was the afternoon, that stretch of time that followed the broth, it had in truth been the dusk. Which at least furnished me with a reason that enabled me to understand the fact that the afternoons had seemed so interminable. I had believed that each stretch of 24 hours divided itself in a natural manner into two halves, the fulcrum marked with the broth. But in actual fact, the fulcrum, if I could still talk of a fulcrum, was marked with the stew and coffee. Or tea.

As I followed this train of ideas, certain other events also took on a different shade. It occurred to me, for instance, that when I had believed the warder and his cronies had come to visit me in the hours of darkness, to search the cell, a time which I believed the warder had chosen so as to disturb what little time I had of rest, that in actual fact this had occurred sometime after dawn. And likewise, that when I'd had the bad dream in the hours of darkness, it had not been in the hours of darkness at all, for it had occurred sometime after the dawn. Yet this did not make it into a dawn reverie as such, at least not as far as I am concerned. In fact, there wasn't in truth a word for such a dream – a bad one, that is – that occurs in the hours after dawn, or if there were I didn't have it at hand, nor did I have access to a thesaurus with which to check. Perchance one can talk of dawnmares, but, to be sure, I have never heard the word.

As I follow this train of disorientated ideas, all of a sudden the man from the next cell starts to tak once more. His tak-tak I had come to associate with the dusk, whereas in fact it occurs after the dawn.

H-O-W-A-R-E-Y-O-U?

So as not to confuse matters, I lie.

M-U-C-H-A-S-U-S-U-A-L.

I don't have the resources to elucidate for him the convoluted events of this interminable and wearisome stretch of time, in which I now realise I have been awake most of the hours of darkness, more or less. Politeness rather than contriteness makes me throw the ball back.

Y-O-U-R-S-E-L-F?

N-O-T-S-O-B-A-D, he answers.

In truth I don't have much to communicate to him this dusk. This dawn, I mean. I feel rather disorientated. It's understandable. In addition, I find his conversation rather dull, to be honest, and I've started to tire of his cross-examinations. Moreover, I have a hunch that he's the kind I would cross the street to avoid in the normal world. Then, as if to confirm this, comes his next.

M-I-S-S-M-E-N-D-O-Y-O-U?

That'll serve me. Serve me! Shouldn't have left the ball in his court. I lob it back.

W-H-A-T-D-O-Y-O-U-M-E-A-N?

Pluck hasn't deserted me, then. Haven't lost that. His turn.

Y-O-U-K-N-O-W-Y-O-U-L-I-T-T-L-E-W-H-O-R-E.

I don't answer. It's understandable. But now he's off he won't let it lie.

S-E-X.

That's what he taks next. Just like that. As if he'd been asked to elucidate the nature of the brand behind Madonna.

S-I-X?

That's me. And once more.

S-I-X-O-F-W-H-A-T?

S-I-X-O-F-T-H-E-F-U-C-K-I-N-G-B-E-S-T.

I should have seen it. What's that?

A-N-D-T-H-E-N-A-G-O-O-D-P-U-L-L-O-N-M-Y-P-E-N-I-S.

What a charmer!

A-G-O-O-D-F-U-C-K-I-N-G.

A silence. I don't know whether to turn a deaf ear to him or tell him to fuck off. Decide on the latter.

G-E-T-S-T-U-F-F-E-D!

He answers.

I-T-S-Y-O-U-N-E-E-D-S-T-U-F-F-I-N-G!

Predictable. I leave it there. Cut one's losses. He taks on, nonetheless. More obscenities. If it were a call I could at least slam the receiver down. Here I haven't the means. I let him run on with it. Decide not to decode what he's on about. Let him tak till he's exhausted with it. He'll soon tire. Like me. It's not much after dawn, but I'm exhausted. I'd doze off in no time if I made an effort. And I would think it won't be forever till lunch. The broth. No, stew. Stew and coffee. Or tea. I check the hole. Still closed. Good. Stick the blindfold on. Tak-tak! Drift into a doze. Tit-tit!

Krrriinnnn! Krrriinnnn! Krrriinnnn! Jesus! *Krrrïinnnn! Krrrïinnnn!* OK! I'm on the case! The warder once more, with the breakfast. No. Lunch. Is that it? Broth and bread. No. That was lunch. Or I used to think it was. Quick, check the blindfold. Fine. *Krrrïinnnn!* Now, take the mess tin. Crawl over...oof!...to the...oof!...door. And I used to think I could do it in half-awake! That's it. Now into the hatch. I hear him ladle it in. Back it comes. It's the coffee, or tea, not broth at all. Of course. Coffee and stew. That's the lunchtime deal from now on. Or tea and stew. Which is it then? Let's see. Hmm. Difficult to tell in actual fact. It doesn't have milk in. But that doesn't clinch it. Could be it's a mixture of the two, swilled around with God knows what else in a colossal vat. *Krrrïinnnn!* Christ! He's in a rush this afternoon! Quick. Drink it down before he loses his cool. *Oooch!* Quite hot this afternoon. There we are. Into the hatch. That's it. Hear him ladle in the broth. Here it comes once more. Tuck in. No, not broth. Stew. That's it. Stew that tastes like oats. Sole difference in fact is it's a bit thinner. Bit more salt. At least when one likens it to the stuff that's served here. Stuff in the normal world another matter. Whatever, scoff it down. For all the benefit it does. Arrests the rumbles in the stomach for an hour or two. There. Good.

Now. What now? It's the afternoon. What shall I do with it? Too tired for a walk. Save that for another time. What, then? Some kind of intellectual exercise to start with. To concentrate the mind. Take me down to earth after all the excitement. Hmmm. I know. Have a bash at that little bit of theatre. Translate it. Into Castilian, for instance. See if I can still do it. Let's have a look now.

– UNA VACA DE LATÓN.
– LE CONVINO A EDGARDO A MARAVILLA.
– ¡DIOS!
– SU JEZEBEL IMPERIAL, MATADA EL LUNES PASADO.
– NINGUNA NECROLOGÍA.
– DESNUCADO. LA REINA ROSA SOLLOZABA.
– MINÚSCULO FURGÓN DE POMPAS FÚNEBRES, ¿QUÉ?
– JUVENTUD XENÓFOBA.
– ZEITGEIST.

Not bad, when all's considered. And without the Collins. Sounds better in Castilian somehow. More of a bounce. *Una vaca de latón*. Yet it would be difficult if I tried to maintain the A-Z backbone, I think. Still, it's an achievement of sorts. Even the achievement of a little task here can make one feel better. Can't think of its like in the normal world. Perchance when one walks into an interview and is told one has secured it before one even sits down. Or if one does *The Times* crossword in record time, without corrections.

*

The warder's been in to see me once more. Came in the door without so much as a knock – I couldn't believe it! – and marched over to where I sat on the bed in the dark. Stroke of luck I had the blindfold on. Here's some chocolate, he said. Then he threw it on the bed. No elucidation. It could be that the Colonel thinks it's one's dies natalis? Perchance it is, who knows? Yet this could be another routine that now I encounter for the first time. After a certain time in the clink the warder comes with some chocolate. To lift the soul. Let one know one's still alive. That the warder still cares. Bollocks does he. Rots one's teeth as well, does chocolate. At least teeth like mine. Above all when not brushed as often as needs be. Sorted, kids born now. Do them with that Fischer stuff after the first few months. No toothache forever after. Unless the bacteria can evolve to breed in this new environment. Learn to chew artificial teeth. Wonderful, if one thinks about it. The marvels of modern science! Never did much for me, however. He didn't offer much else. Just turned and left.

Not so much as a fare-thee-well. Mind, I'm one to talk. I didn't even utter a thanks. But then I have reasons. I don't think he can have noticed much out of whack with the door this time, for he went out at once. Little ruse must have worked, then. Good. That's one little success however one cuts it. Chalk that one on the board.

The chocolate. Quick. Off with the blindfold and let's have a look at it. See what make it is to start with. Hmm. Hard to tell. It's in an unmarked box. No doubt standard clink issue. Or could be Red Cross. But then one would reckon on a little red cross on the box, wouldn't one? Or at least some kind of indication, a communication of some kind.

DON'T WORRY!
WE'RE DOING ALL WE CAN TO GET YOU OUT OF THERE!
ENJOY YOUR CHOCOLATE!

But no such luck. Let's have a look, whatever. See what's on offer. I sit on the bed and count out the number of bars, then the number of bits of chocolate in each bar. 6 bars. 18 bits of chocolate a bar. That's, let's see, that makes 108 bits of chocolate. Sufficient for 36 bits over 24 hours for 3 stretches of 24 hours, that's 2 bars in each 24 hours, or 18 bits in 24 hours for 6 stretches of 24 hours, that's a bar for each stretch of 24 hours. On a theoretical level, of course, I could make them last for an even more extended time. Such as 9 bits for each 24 hours for 12 stretches of 24 hours, or 3 bits for each 24 hours for 36 stretches of 24 hours, or one bit for each 24 hours for 108 stretches of 24 hours. Or if I had no more than one bit for each 3 lots of 24 hours it would last me 324 lots of 24 hours, that's almost an annum! But let's not be defeatist. I could be out of here before that. And whatever the case, the chocolate would have become stale before then. That's if it hasn't done before now. Let's see.

At once I devour 6 bits. Can't decide whether it's stale or rubbish chocolate. For certain, it's not Swiss chocolate, so can't be Red Cross. Unless the Red Cross too need to economise and have outsourced. I devour 6 more. Still can't tell, but it does the business, calms the wild animal that chews at the heart of the stomach. I eat 6 more. That's the first bar done. Then at once I devour another bar. To tell the truth, the diet here is so minimal that I could in all likelihood devour all 108 bits, all 6 bars in other words, and still make no real difference. Yet I'd chunder, for sure. Even after two bars I still have room for more. When one is handed extras here one's stomach stretches in accordance. When it has been on such a short tether for such a time it balloons at the first convenience, if that makes sense. Still, I won't have more chocolate for now. I'll hide it under the mattress. At the back. There. That should do it. Pretend it's not there, like I do with the bread sometimes. Whatever, I estimate that the broth will arrive soon. The broth with its ration of bread, which for so much time I believed came at noon, whereas in fact the warder comes with it at dusk. After all, it would be wise to leave room for it. Starvation is the best sauce.

Just as I reach this conclusion I feel the ache in back of the mouth. In the back tooth with the hole. I touch it. *Oooaieee!* The tooth is even and smooth once more, the chocolate has made its home in the hole where the fill-in once was. I see if I can lick it out. No use. What could I use to clean it out, then? I need a toothbrush for sure. Or a cocktail stick. No chance of that in here! I have another lick, bathe it in saliva. In the end it softens, melts, runs out. Once more, the stab of irritation. *Oooaiee!* I lick round the hole. Feels worse now, but I don't see how it can be. Unless a bit more has fallen out and I didn't notice. In for a kick, in for a kill, as is often said. I'll swill it with water in a minute. It needs to be clean. Have to remember to be careful with it from now on. Above all with the chocolate. The broth, at least, should be OK. The bread too, but it could be wise to dunk it. I'll do that. It will make a nice variation.

When I reach the sink, all of a sudden I remember the dormouse. I take a bit of chocolate out. Make an effort to feed it. Fail. It isn't interested. I coax it. *Num-num-num!* I wave the chocolate in front of its nose. *Numanumanumnum!* But it's no use. Just not interested. Which is not what I wished for. You'd think it would have been ravenous. Too bad. I turn the faucet on. Start to fill the mess tin. Just as I do so the warder comes with the broth. *Krrriinnnn! Krrriinnnn!* I ditch the water, leave him to hammer while I crawl over to the door. Usual routine. The hatch. The mess tin in. The mess tin filled. Then back. I take the bread, remember to dunk it, make it soft. Tastes better like that, too, even if the broth is the same as ever. Lettuce and water. Quite thin. Tastes of seaweed. I bolt it down. As usual.

*

Had to make a dash for the bucket. Just made it and teased the trousers off, stuck to the backside as these are like velcro, when out it all came like a mudslide. Sloshed onto the sides and over. Then to make matters worse the rim subsided. Krriick! Sloooosh! Pffflottt! I clambered out as best I could then washed down, and tried hard not to interfere with the mouse. The smell is terrible, the flies will have a whale of a time. Christ! I still feel awful too. Please God it's not diarrhoea. The warder could have adulterated the food. In an effort to break the little resistance I have left. The warders do that sometimes. Perchance I've said so before. Bastards. Well, the sods can break down one's bowels, but the bastards won't break me. I'm made of sterner stuff than that.

I lie down on the bed. Ease the blindfold off. If the warder comes in and sees me like this, then to be honest I couldn't care less. After a while I become accustomed to the smell. Like the man in La Fontaine and the tanner's. You become accustomed to all sorts after a while, as far as I can see. Custom reconciles us to all. That's it! The maxim I was after. Knew it would come to me in the end. With the trowel of solitude we unearth the roots of truth.

*

I think I must have snoozed off for a while. When I came to I felt a little better. Not much, but a little all the same. Whatever, I had sufficient motivation to have another root around the cell. See what I could find. After a while I started to look once more at the bits of old broadsheets and the articles I had torn from the walls, and in their midst I found the last few soiled leaves of a book of Sir James Jeans's on a theoretical idea he referred to as Planck's constant. I don't know what made me look at it in the first instance, the hard sciences have never been of enormous interest to me, as I fail to understand their most basic ideas and calculations as a rule, but I started to read it all the same and found that with a little concentration I was able to follow its thesis in the dimness of the cell. The book was no doubt aimed at novices, but that was all one to me. What stuck out for me, in brief, was a remark Sir James made in the conclusion to the effect that Planck had demonstrated the existence of what he called a unit of atomicness to which no material idea could be attached. He had shown, in other words, or so the author maintained, that the smallest and most irreducible measurement in the material world was not of a minute atom nor of a diminutive wave, but of an ethereal substance which he called, in an effort to find the correct word, an action, which had no material form to offer to the scientific mind. The author shaded this observation when he went on to admit that it was difficult to determine at this time when definitive evidence would be found. It could be, he went on, that we have uncovered no more than a corner of the sketch. While this was, in actual fact, no more than a common observation, it occurred to me that it could be said to describe what we with blandness refer to as the known. For we are forever in one of two conditions. Either we claim to know with assurance, in which case we are sure to have a successor who will contradict us, both in science and in life, or, on the other hand, we admit that what we know is uncertain.

The second condition, it seems to me, is the more honest. For while we act most of the time as if what we know were final, and as if the forces which motivate us and all we did were therefore as clear as the waters in a stream, in actual fact we crawl around in darkness. In this, our contract with the known, enshrined as it is in our habits of education, resembles the manner in which the mole burrows under the earth. She enters the earth at the location she chooses, and she burrows until she comes out at another location. If we had moles who burrowed into the centre of the earth and came out on the other side, these moles would still come out on the same surface. If such action, therefore, is like our education, the discovered surface is like the known. There forever seems to be an unburrowed desert around the location of the exit.

Do I take it all too far in the end? Is it not that it resembles the case of an inmate like me, in a cell like this, and no more? No, I think not. In the world outside it's no different. One's command of idiolects, for instance. Extensive, but limited. Ever since Babel we have had access to no more than inexact information. And even before that it can't have been much different. If the architect had understood the fall-out, he wouldn't have continued with the tower. But he didn't know what the result would be. Therefore his information must have been limited. Forever no more than limited.

These trains of ideas run off with me sometimes. As now, for instance. Just run off into the distance, as if under their own steam. Perchance that's what folk call them trains for? I don't know. Whatever the case, this brain of mine isn't often so fertile. Or so it seems to me. At times like this. It could be this leisure (*leisure!*) without end. For I can devote as much time to these words as the resources of the brain allow. And if I wander into thinkers' territories at times I don't care two hoots. Yet. Yet. I still hanker after books. Still more after notebook and ink. A futile wish for fixedness, it could be said. But it would let me avoid the habit I fall into when I think the same business over and over. Could be I've said that before.

Tak-tak. Tak-tak. There he is once more. The old sod. Well, I think he's old, but he could well not be. Could be a debauchee in his thirties for all I know. Yet it could be taken as normal behaviour in our modern times. Could think I'm the weirdo. God knows! That bit in Freud. Dora, that was it. Man comes in and seizes the woman from behind, then forces her to kiss him. What was it Freud said? How did he write it? This was without doubt the sort of situation to arouse a distinct instinct of sexual excitement in a woman who had never been touched before. Pah! Tak-tak-tak. Don't listen to it. That's the best tack. Just end in another war of words otherwise. Won't do either of us a favour. Not that I care a hoot about him.

Yet somehow I can't turn a deaf ear to it. For I can tell there's a difference this time, at least as far as the tak-tak is concerned. First off, it's not the code we use. Used. It's another one. And more crucial still, it comes from the other side of the room to normal. The side with the bed, that is. As a rule it comes from the side that faces the bed. Quick as I can, I slam both ears to the wall, listen. Yes. It issues from the bedside wall, for sure. Quick, fetch the mess tin.

Tak...tak. That's them on the other side of the wall. I send the ball back. Tak...tak...tak. Three taks, so no-one can think it's an echo. At once there's a burst of taks in answer.

Tak-tak-tak...tak-tak...tak...tak...tak...tak.
Tak-tak...tak...tak.
Tak-tak-tak...tak...tak...tak...tak.
Tak-tak...tak...tak...tak...tak.
Tak-tak-tak...tak-tak-tak.
Tak-tak.
Tak-tak.
Tak-tak-tak...tak-tak...tak...tak...tak.
Tak-tak...tak...tak.

End of communication. I don't understand a word. But he seems to use the double-taks and the tri-taks, even if not in the manner I'm used to. Unless he uses an idiolect which is unknown to me. Or some kind of street-talk. For if he uses the double-taks and the tri-taks in the manner I'm used to, that is a double-tak for ten, and a tri-tak for five, what he's knocked out, unless I'm mistaken, is S-L-I-N-J-J-J-R-L, which doesn't mean much. At least not to me. Nor does it resemble even one of the codes I've come across before. It must be the case, then, that I don't bark at the crown of the correct tree. Bark, tree. Never noticed that before. Odd. I tak once more, twice. Tak...tak. Both to let them know I'm still here, and to embolden them to make the communication once more, let me have another bite at the cherries. He understands what I'm after.

Tak-tak-tak...tak-tak...tak...tak...tak...tak.
Tak-tak...tak...tak.
Tak-tak-tak...tak...tak...tak...tak.
Tak-tak...tak...tak...tak...tak.
Tak-tak-tak...tak-tak-tak.
Tak-tak.
Tak-tak.
Tak-tak-tak...tak-tak...tak...tak...tak.
Tak-tak...tak...tak.

It terminates once more. Not the code I'm used to, but a bit familiar, nonetheless. On a hunch I test it in a different order. Double-tak for five, tri-tak for ten. What does that make? Let's see. Mmmm. S-G-N-I-T-E-E-R-G. Just as bad as before. Unless...unless. *Yes! That's it!* Whole business is reversed. G-R-E-E-T-I-N-G-S! But backwards. Quick as I can I snatch the mess tin, tak back.

O-L-L-E-H! T-I-T-O-G!

Listen. Tri-tak, lone tak. Tri-tak, double-tak. K-O! Tak back the same. We're in business.

I take the bull's horns.

E-M-A-N-R-U-O-Y-S-I-T-A-H-W?

Listen to the answer. A woman's name. Thank God! She asks the same. I tell her. Me once more.

E-R-E-H-N-E-E-B-U-O-Y-E-V-A-H-G-N-O-L-W-O-H?

She's not sure. Seems like a while, she taks. Asks me the same. Same answer, more or less. I tak once more.

R-O-F-N-I-U-O-Y-E-R-A-T-A-H-W?

She doesn't know. Tell her I'm in the same boat.

I ask her other details, or she asks them of me. Date of birth. Married or divorced. Children. Job. Future aims. As it turns out she's a three times divorcee with nine children, all with other men, all male. Used to work for a cleanser manufacturer till she was sacked when she was found with the staff director. After this, it seems, she tried various lines of work. Cleaner. Child minder. Door-to-door work. Underwear and lace. Chambermaid. Adult calls. She was called the Ice-cream Girl. You know I've forever luuuuuved to lick ice-creams ever since I was a little one but now I'm an adult there's one succulent tool I like even more! Claims she'd like to have a little store of her own if she's ever let out.

I ask her.

S-N-A-L-P-E-P-A-C-S-E-Y-N-A-U-O-Y-E-V-A-H?

Await the answer.

S-E-Y.

Y-E-H-T-E-R-A-T-A-H-W?

Her once more.

H-C-U-M-O-O-T-Y-A-S-T-N-A-C.

Then once more.

G-N-I-N-E-T-S-I-L-S-E-N-O-E-M-O-S-E-S-A-C-N-I.

K-O, I answer.

She vows to tell me more tomorrow. Tells me it'll be safer like that. She taks backwards an extended farewell.

T-H-G-I-N-D-O-O-G!

I do likewise.

T-H-G-I-N!

Best snooze I've had in a while in the hours of darkness. Drifted off at once after the communication. Came as a bit of a shock. Would have caused me to be awake till dawn at one time. Above all the idea of a break-out. Must have needed it, I think. I had another dream. Don't remember it with much clearness, however. What was it? Yes. There was a scribe. That's it. It was as if all of a sudden I awoke, I blabbered on as usual, in the brain, and there in the corner of the cell was this scribe. Just as one would envision a scribe. Kind of Old Testament look, it could be said. Fat nose, not much hair, bald, enormous beard which fell down to the floor, and he wore this sort of dark cassock. He must have been sat on a stool, but one couldn't see it. Peradventure he sat on a box. It was covered with the cassock, whatever it was, so one couldn't tell. He must have been able to hear me as well, so that there's little doubt I dictated rather than blabbered inside. For each word I said, that's it, said, he noted down. As fast as I could talk the ink scurried across the book. And whenever I took a breather, he continued for a few moments, to finish what I'd said, I would think, then when he had finished he looked at me, as if he awaited more. When I saw him look at me like that, I had to continue, even if I didn't in actual fact have much left to communicate. I must have recounted more or less the whole kit and caboodle. Situation. Wretchedness of. Room. Dimensions and contents. Cross-examinations. Pastimes. Communications with inmates in nearest cells. And so on. Somehow I had the sense I couldn't tell him sufficient. Wasn't able to articulate the one deed he wanted to hear about. At least that's the notion I had. He didn't talk to me, of that I'm sure. Just sat there and scribbled without so much as a wave, and looked over at me from time to time. That needful look in his face. I'm not sure how the dream ended. It was no doubt a slow fade kind of affair. Whatever the case, it wasn't the kind of dream from which one awoke in a cold sweat. Just came and went in the hours of darkness. But it must have been rather forceful to leave a mark. At least, I could remember it, after a little effort, more or less, at dawn.

I think it's all connected with the desire for ink and a notebook. An inner wish to write all this down, when in actual fact I don't even utter it out loud. Daren't. Just let it all run around the brain. I surmise from this that I must think that to write it all down would endow it with a kind of existence, which it doesn't have now, and also a kind of nobleness, which it doesn't have either. Make the whole business into a kind of internment notebook. *A Detainee's Memoirs*. Tell the world how I met with discrimination incarnate and led a valiant battle to remain sane. Won out in the face of adverse circumstances, and all that.

Must be one of those wish fulfilment dreams, I think. For, now I think of it, there's more to these sentences than the mere need to fill in the time. It is true that I don't write them down, it is true too that I don't utter them out loud, but that doesn't mean I can't frame them as if I wrote them down, as if I uttered them out loud. To be sure, sometimes I act as if I addressed another human, a listener or a reader, it doesn't much matter in the end, whereas in actual fact I don't do that at all, do I? There I am at it once more! One does no other than talk to oneself, in silence, in the dark. Put a reel-to-reel recorder in the cell, switch it on, leave it there. At the close of business it will have recorded not a word. Sometimes, too, one tells oneself about events which have occurred but a moment since – mundane actions, like when the orderlies come in, or when the warder comes to the door, with the oats, or the stew, or the broth, or when I visit the bucket, or what's left of it – sometimes one tells oneself about these deeds in the historic tense, after the event, as if one recited a tale to someone, a tale which is now over and done with, as if one recounted the sack of Thebes or some such. When in actual fact this tale isn't over. It carries on. I can't even remember how it started, and I haven't a clue how it will end.

But what if I do break out some time? All this would come in useful then. Kind of exordial work. I'd be met at the station with a team of news men and women, who'd all scream out for the tale, make me offers for it too, then the bits I'd worked on in the historic tense I could offer verbatim. The other bits I could remodel as needs demanded. Then there'd be the book manufacturers, who'd all vie with each other for the exclusive tale. All I'd have to do would be to add a little historical detail, embellish the cross-examination scenes a bit, add a torture scene or two, the electric chair, the rack, the Sicilian bull, or some such device, that should hold their attention, then finish it off, add a moral at the end, Affliction comes with instruction in its hand, that sort of contrivance, and that would be it! Quids in! Could be an idea to mention to the Colonel? Offer him a cut and he could even find a means to send me back home! He'd be able to refurbish the cells. Concrete over the floors. Put tiles down, even. Then he could take a rise, the Governor and the Lieutenant too, who knows, even the warder, set new standards in institutional salaries. Fix themselves with five-star retirement schemes and life insurance. The whole institution could have an overhaul, in a word. And all thanks to me! Privatisation could be next. Advertise. Rebrand. Have a whole load of clients like me each month. The scheme would rake it in ! Have to branch out after a while. Start a franchise, even. Then move into other areas. Residential weekends. Contests, to devise new forms of torture. That sort of stuff.

*

Krrreennnn! Krrreennnn! At last the warder arrives with the breakfast. I'd started to think he hadn't remembered me. Usual routine. The hatch. The mess tin in. Then filled. And so on. Usual cold oats. Bolt them down, as usual. Still famished, as usual. If I ever do the book I'll have to embellish a little here. Think of a better menu. Choice of cakes to start with, with fresh fruit and tea or coffee. Various salads, cheeses, bread and suchlike for lunch, avoid the over-elaborate. Then later on, a five-course à la carte menu with wine list. Indicative menu could be:

ENTRÉE

Lobster

or

Colchester Mussels

or

Crudités

MAIN COURSE

Stuffed Chicken
or
Hare in Guinness
or
Trout with Almonds
or
Chef's Choice

SALAD

Watercress and Walnut
or
Globe Artichoke with Garlic and Herb Coulis
or
Chef's Salad

DESSERT

Lemon Sorbet
or
Chocolate Charlotte
or
Strawberries and Cream
or
Pear Crumble

CHEESEBOARD

Munster
or
Brie
or
Red Leicester
or
Hand-crafted Cheddar
or
Livarot
or
Stilton

The whole lot washed down with a bottle of Montrachet Blanc '66, and finished with a nice Calvados and a coffee. Could even do a cookbook as a kind of tie-in if the memoirs took off. *The Prison Gourmet*. Nice shot of me on the front in a chef's hat with an inmate's uniform and a ball and chain round the left ankle. Ghost-written, of course, but no harm in that. Plum in the middle of these future schemes when in comes the warder. Doesn't even bother to knock. Stroke of luck I had the blindfold on. Get off that arse, he announces. Tells me the Governor wants a word. Took me to the room with the little man behind the wide table. That's the Governor, the little man, I must have said that. The others were all here and correct. The Colonel, the Lieutenant, Gore. The Colonel asked me to sit down, so I did. Let me take the blindfold off too. Almost rather have left it on, the illumination in there was so intense. Not used to it now, these little mole beads, not at all. I sat there, looked at the floor. Waited for one of them to talk. The ball was in their court. After all, the Colonel had wanted to see me and not vice versa. The Governor asked me if all was OK with me. If I was comfortable in the accommodation. Accommodation! That's a fine word for it. Yes, I said. Lied. He beamed at me, then, as he fiddled with his ear, asked me if I had made advances with the work on the behavioural habits of moles. I told him that the fieldwork was almost finished, but that soon I'd need to start to write it out. That I'd need notebooks, ink, a calculator if it was available. The Colonel frowned. And from where did I think I would obtain these items? he asked. I looked him in the face, and said that I had assumed that it would not be outside the remit of the Governor himself, who had been so kind as to take an interest in the work, to obtain them on an inmate's behalf. The Governor and the Colonel traded looks. Then all of a sudden the Governor abandoned his seat and told me I could leave. If I behaved, he said, he'd see what he could do about the notebook and ink.

The warder shoved me from behind and escorted me out. I think the Colonel, had he been free to exert his will, would have handed me over to Gore. For while I had reason to be content, since there was no doubt I had won a little battle in there on this occasion, whether or not the ink and notebooks ever materialised, it was a battle which had been won at his cost. I don't think he can have been blind to this. As I was escorted out of the room, Gore looked me over, with hatred, from head to toe. He still carried his truncheon in his left hand, thick and black with a smooth head, with which he beat the side of his trousers from time to time. Still no hole visible in them. At least on this occasion he won't have the chance to use it, not on me at least. It was obvious that he was miffed about this and disliked the lenient treatment I seemed to be allowed. Peradventure he was even a little envious of the unusual bond which seemed to be in evidence between me and the Governor? While his line of work was to break the inmates, I think he must still have harboured some hidden admiration for those who resisted.

*

Back in the cell I've waited such an extended time for the warder to come with the lunch that I've reached the conclusion I must have missed it. In the cross-examination. Pointless to shed tears over lost milk, to be sure. I use both hands to root around under the mattress in an effort to find the uneaten bars of chocolate which I stashed there some time back. Then, lo and behold, I don't uncover the chocolate alone, but the biscuits too, or what remains of them. For I can feel with the hands that some creature or other has had a nibble at them. No doubt another mouse. For where there's one mouse, in this inmate's ken, there are bound to be others. Unlike moles, mice are not unsociable creatures. And breed like rabbits. Nonetheless, I take a bite from one of the biscuits. These seem to have become stale to boot, so I crawl over to the corner where the bucket stands, stood rather, and ditch them. This can be our little mulcher from now on. It stinks, but at least it should maintain the cell's warmth in the hours of darkness. Almost as soon as I've done so, I realise the mistake. I should have remembered the dormouse, who'd no doubt have welcomed a few biscuit crumbs. For sure, his friends seem to have taken to them. But it's too late. What's done cannot be undone, as is often said.

There are now four bars of chocolate left. That's 72 bits. 18 bits each 24 hours for 4 lots of 24 hours, that's one bar each 24 hours, or, more realistic, 36 bits each 24 hours for 2 lots of 24 hours, that's 2 bars each 24 hours. Pointless to make them last for ever. I don't know for what stretch of time I'll be in here. And besides, I don't want the chocolate to deteriorate. At once, then, I devour the two bars for the first 24 hours. Still famished, so I scoff one of tomorrow's as well. Feel a little better for it. Should make me less ravenous for an hour or two, at least. The unconsumed bar I stash in the recess, out of the reach of the mice. Even if the mice didn't touch it, and seemed to like the stale biscuits more, even if I know the dormouse turned it down, I don't want to take risks when I don't have to. Better safe and sure.

Got time to kill now. The afternoon stretches before me like a week without bread. I lie back on the bed. Run over the hobbies I've invented. As a starter exercise I have a bash at a few maxims. Reconstruct a few common ones.

A Scotsman's throne is his arsehole.
If the faucet leaks swear at it.
Where there's a till there's a thief.
The trend obfuscates the teens.
Time wounds old heels.
The more taste the less tweed.
Clever tell lie.
The streets of London are lined with the old.

Not bad. Some better than others, for sure. But not bad all the same. Have to do that over sometime. Yet it took more time than one would think. It must be about time for another walk. Choose Barcelona. Wander.

As I leave the shade of a narrow street, I stroll into the hot sunshine of the Plaça Portal de la Pau, behind which stretches the old harbour. On the left the Columbus Monument, built for the Universal Exhibition of 1888, towers over us, as if it were there to commemorate the achievements of an astronaut rather than those of a sailor and adventurer. About 30 metres above its base the column is enshrouded with a thin evanescent cloud which trails off to the left, the direction which Columbus indicates with his raised arm. A 737 descends, low, over the water, and from where I stand its route seems to intersect with the head of the column, so that, for an instant, the hand of Columbus seems to touch the tail of the aircraft, and at the same instant the monument comes to resemble an enormous letter E, which stands at the limit of the town. A moment later, the aircraft has vanished.

On the left lies the start of the Ramblas, the sinuous central street which delineates the heart of the conurbation. In actual fact it consists of five individual streets, but each one flows into the next. Its successive names – the Ramlas, the Ramelas, the Rambellar – are all deformations of the Arabic ramla, for torrent, and it is said that in former times the Ramblas marked the course of a seasonal river, whose channel was used as a road in the arid season.

The central tree-lined track is crowded at this hour. Dead ahead of me an old traveller woman, who wears a headscarf to shield herself from the blaze of the sun, sits at a little trestle table, where she stares into her fortune-teller's ball. A red-haired woman in her twenties, hid behind Foster Grants, is seated across from her, and listens with a cocked ear to the woman's disclosures, which she delivers in a voice too muffled for all but her client to hear. Around them have coalesced a small band of adults and children, who, like the traveller, stare into the fortune-teller's ball. The band consists of some nineteen individuals, ten adults and nine or so children, but its exact constitution alters from time to time as different individuals arrive or leave. Further on, other entertainers and artistes each do their best to attract the interest of tourists with their acts. There are cabaret artists, sword-swallowers, flamenco dancers and musicians. A man with a camera invites children to have their shot taken with a dwarf albino simian which sits on his shoulder. Performance artists stick narrow bands of torn news-sheets to the trunk of a tree with flour and water. An old man in white boots entertains a small crowd with his flea circus. Close at hand, a suited man with a drunk's red nose (fake?) intones Guantanamera in a falsetto voice (fake?) to the sound of a ukulele. A trio of lutenists who wear straw hats and bandannas strum to the sound of castanets. A violinist bows extracts from Vivaldi's *Four Seasons*. There are also stalls that sell broadsheets, leather belts, souvenirs, cakes and sweets. One individual stall sells local varieties of chocolate; its forte is Xocolata BLANXART, a brand which contains the constituents cocoa, sucrose and vanilla alone. On the off-white cardboard sheath, in black ink, in the form of a traditional woodcut, a character is shown in C16th costume – flat black shoes, hose, a tradesman's smock and a small disciform hat. He kneels over a small oval table, and seems to strain chocolate into small round moulds from an item which resembles an outsized carrot, or the snout of a mole, which in actual fact must be a crude kind of cake decorator's nozzle.

Near at hand there are kiosks which sell live canaries, rabbits, exotic fish and native shrubs. There are counterfeit smokes from itinerant street vendors, and brooches and necklaces stretched out on blankets on the soil. All around there are folk who sit at the outdoor tables of cafés and restaurants, who make conversation with friends or read the news, *El País* and *El Periódico*. "¿Has sentit les notícies de l'ETA?" someone asks. "¿Beurem a la Fundació Miró?" asks another.

I leave the Ramblas for a moment for the relative calm of the Plaça Reial. Laid out around 1850, it is studded with trees whose leaves resemble the outstretched human hand, a feature from which the trees derive their common name, and intricate decorated iron street furniture created in the atelier of the adolescent Gaudi, and bordered with fashionable arcaded mansions. At its centre stands a stone fountain around which have clustered an assortment of down-and-outs, travellers, bikers, and bearded Catalan eccentrics, who barter chitchat and smokes, as all the while a half-drunk bottle of second-rate wine is shuffled from hand to hand. As I enter their orbit one of them asks if

I have some extra cash. "¿Qualsevol canvi de recanvi?" "I am a traveller, not a bank," I answer, which fails to have the desired effect. With a firm hold on wallet and satchel, I resist the allure of the smart arcaded cafés, walk around the fountain, then take the cut that leads back to the Ramblas, and walk once more in a direction which leaves the harbour behind me.

I walk in front of a chic café that swarms with tourists and locals alike, which faces the Gran teatre del Liceu, one of Barcelona's most celebrated artistic venues. Founded in the mid-C19th, it soon became a bastion of the commercial and intellectual classes, and was devastated in 1893 when an Anarchist, who wanted to even the score after the execution of a comrade, threw two fire-bombs into the stalls in the middle of a rendition of *William Tell.* It has since been restored to its former illustriousness and now, as a result of the modernista enthusiasm for *Tristan und Isolde*, it has become the world's most renowned centre for renditions of this masterwork, and other works from the same inimitable source, outside the GDR. Behind it is hidden the warren of run-down hotels and insalubrious hostales, ill-lit clubs and sex stores, ill-lit bars and laundromats, their clothes hoisted back and forth across the airless streets, which in combination form the Barri Xinès or Chinese Quarter which features in the work of Jean Genet.

A short while afterwards, before I reach the indoor market with its stacks of exotic fruit and artichokes, swordfish and meat, I turn off down a narrow side street which takes me into the heart of the Barri Gòtic or Gothic Quarter with its ancient and narrow streets, its Cathedral and its famous bakeries and restaurants. A thief, crutch tucked under his arm, hobbles down the street, as he rifles the contents of a stolen wallet. He discards cards, I.D., tickets, whatever he can find in actual fact, save the banknotes, which he twists into a roll and thrusts down his loose trousers, and the coins, which he slides into the bottom of his mouth. At once, I feel for the wallet. Yes. Still there. Thank God! Won't have a re-run of the last visit, then. All those hours with the Guardia Civil. Makes one feel like the criminal oneself. All of a sudden I am struck with the decorated window of a small modernista cake store, the Patisseria Gaudi. The centre of the window is filled with an enormous chocolate cake in the form of Gaudi's celebrated modernista cathedral, its domes mounted with silver balls, and which bears, white on black, the letters HOSANNA IN EXCELSIS. At its feet lie numerous smaller edible cathedrals, in luminous surreal colours of red, vermilion, blue and violet. On shelves there are other cakes, all moulded into the forms of different Gaudi monuments: a lizard from the Parc Güell, a scale model of the Palau de la Música Catalana, the lizard from the roof of the Casa Batllo, and details in white chocolate from the Palau Güell, the Casa Teixidor and elsewhere. There is also the more usual selection of biscuits, croissants and cakes.

Attracted more to the latter than the rococo inventiveness of the Gaudi cakes, I shove on the door and stand in line. In front of me a woman with manicured nails indicates in a conceited manner the cakes she wants delivered. On her shoulder rests a small snakeskin sack, from one end of which the head of a diminutive Chihuahua, which seems to be at rest, sticks out. A notice in the window, which shows a boot that kicks a Poodle into the air, reads: ¡Gossos Prohibits! I remain silent. Let mutts at rest lie. When I reach the counter I ask for an ensaimada, hide it in the satchel, and leave.

A minute later the street leads me to the haven of Santa Maria del Pi, surrounded with its sunlit vistas. Here I take a seat on the shaded terrace of a small wood-fronted bar and do the best I can to catch the attention of the smart waiter as he hurries between the tables. In front of the bar a tattered trad trio (alto sax, clarinet, double bass) bash out an instrumental version of Bourbon Street Parade. Across from them a street theatre collective enacts the tale of Saint Jordi and the firedrake, in translation for the tourists, with marionettes. Saint Jordi, astride a horse, announces his noble antecedents and his fearlessness before the bold firedrake. Enter firedrake.

> Who's he that seeks the firedrake's blood
> And calls so ireful and so loud?
> That Greek mastiff will he before me stand;
> I'll cut him down with this valiant hand.

With curvèd teeth and scabrous claw
Of such I'd devour half a score
And hold this stomach till I'd more.

The marionettes run around. There are cries of affliction, roars of wrath and, which strikes me as odd, the clash of steel on steel. There is a billow of smoke. Saint Jordi has killed the firedrake.

To the left, two American women talk in loud voices about their travels and adventures. "The clubs are terrific," one announces. "But what the hell's that weird dance about?" "When in Rome...," another answers. "Els turistes tornaran a casa aviat," intones another. The waiter arrives. I ask him for a café con leche and a box of matches. I take a——

Krrreennnn! Krrreennnn! Just as I start to look forward to a real coffee, the excursion is cut short with the arrival of the broth and bread. Usual routine. The mess tin. The hatch. Into the hatch. Then back once more. I bolt them down, as usual. Still famished, as usual. I lie down on the bed. Let the food settle. I think about the time that I was in Barcelona when Franco was still in the ascendent. Police with revolvers on each street corner. The time I was shot at as we drove over the border. The Guardia aim at the wheels, the driver had said. I hadn't been so sure. Then it occurs to me that the best contrivance to make the food settle is to stand. I take the blindfold off, check the hole, then walk the room from side to side. Total of 60 times. Have a bash at some more maxims while I'm at it. There's no bloke without ire. A God is for Christmas, not for life. That should do it. Lie back on the bed. Unfill the mind. Relax.

*

Tak...tak. Tak...tak. The woman. Must be her once more. In the next cell. Quick. Get the mess tin. Tak back. Tak...tak...tak. Three times, so she doesn't think it's an echo. I set the ball in motion.

O-L-L-E-H!

Get the formalities over with. Then onto the exit scheme with a bit of luck. She taks back.

N-I-A-G-A-O-L-L-E-H! U-O-Y-E-R-A-W-O-H?

I lie, tell her I'm fine. In fact I feel terrible. Too much chocolate earlier on, I think. I can feel some of it now, still inside the mouth. Stuck in the molar hole. I ask her the same. Same answer, more or less. Good. At least that's over, then. Nosiness drives me on. I can't hold back a moment more. Dive in.

S-N-A-L-P-E-P-A-C-S-E-E-H-T-N-O-S-W-E-N-Y-N-A?

Her.

Y-R-R-O-W-T-N-O-D. W-O-N-U-O-Y-L-L-E-T-N-A-C-I. E-T-A-L-O-O-T-E-B-L-L-I-W-W-O-R-R-O-M-O-T.

Me.

Y-A-W-A-E-R-I-F!

So she starts her extended and elaborate backwards elucidation, scattered with breaks now and then to be sure I understand all the details. Tomorrow, she tells me, is outside exercise. It comes round once a month. News to me, but mum's the word. We'll be taken to the exercise field, she tells me. In a van. It lies some ten kilometres from the slammer. That's about six miles, I estimate.

N-E-H-T-T-A-H-W?

That's me. She taks back.

T-I-B-T-N-A-T-R-O-P-M-I-E-H-T-S-I-S-I-H-T.

Tells me to listen. And remember. She won't be able to reiterate it tomorrow. Once we reach the exercise field, she continues, we'll all be let out of the van, or vans, for there's a kind of fleet of them. All the inmates, the orderlies, the warders, and the bosses. The Colonel. The Lieutenant. The Governor. Then comes the all-ball, she adds.

L-L-A-B-L-L-A? I ask.

L-L-A-B-L-L-A-S-E-Y, she announces. S-R-E-D-R-A-W-S-U-S-R-E-V-S-R-E-N-O-S-I-R-P.

She runs over the rules of allball, a kind of variation on baseball, but with more sizeable teams. Then she describes the exercise field. It is bordered with a tall wall, it seems, which is concealed at one end from the view of the Colonel. It's he who looks after surveillance, it seems. All the others muck in, bar a few warders. From where he stands, this is the crucial bit, a section of the wall is concealed, or to some extent concealed, for the field sinks down in one corner and forms a hollow. This area is near third base. Now she elucidates the scheme. I'll take first strike. Somehow I have to make it to second base. She'll then take second strike. Get herself to second base while I run on to third. When the next inmate takes the strike, we both run like hell for the wall. Me in a direct line. Her via third base. When we reach the wall, she tells me – if we reach it, for there are Alsatians it would seem, and the Colonel carries a rifle – a marline ladder will be lobbed over from the other side. I ask the obvious.

E-M-O-C-W-O-H?

She tells me she has contacts. Too convoluted to describe in detail.

K-O, I answer.

Once we're over the wall a car will be there for us. If all runs to schedule we climb in and drive to freedom. I cut in.

E-V-I-R-D-T-N-A-C-I!

K-O-S-T-I, she tells me. R-U-E-F-F-U-A-H-C-A-E-B-L-L-E-R-E-H-T.

That's the break-out then. In a nutshell. More or less, as she laid it out.

S-N-O-I-T-S-E-U-Q-Y-N-A? she asks.

I can think of several. Ask the first.

E-R-E-H-T-T-O-N-S-R-A-C-E-H-T-F-I-T-A-H-W?

L-L-E-H-E-K-I-L-N-U-R!

K-O, I answer. Her once more.

S-N-O-I-T-S-E-U-Q-R-E-H-T-O-Y-N-A?

I lie, tell her no. She makes me run over the whole kit-and-caboodle once more. Just to make sure I've remembered it all. I have. More or less. She taks backwards her extended farewell. I do the same.

Can't seem to doze off. That backwards tak-tak-tak

still hammers out in the head. And I'm excited about the idea of a break-out too. Need to calm down. Get some rest if I'm to be fit for tomorrow. I run over an A-Z of famous versifiers. Soft into the arms of Somnus.

Ariosto	
Blake	
Chaucer	
Donne	
Eliot	
Frost	Poems: that which can't be translated.
Gautier	
Herbert	
?????????	Can't think. Have to invent one.
Isbister	A minor C20th versifier. Friend of Thomas. Now well in his nineties.
Johnson	
Keats	
Lowell	What was it he said about the lumen at the end of the tunnel? Could be a train!

Mallarmé
Nerval

Owen

Petrarch

Quasimodo

Rochester

Swift

Dearest lord, it's a difficult task,
For a man to wait here,
unable to ask.

Traherne

Unamuno

Verlaine

Words

Got no rest at all in the dark hours. Farted around like a Jack-in-the-box, with endless visits to the toilet or what's left of it. Toilet area would be a more fit characterisation, I think. Bad wind too. Abstinence makes the fart blow like a fender. I've come to the conclusion that it must have been the chocolate. No doubt the reason the mice weren't interested. Sixth sense. No doubt what the boss meant when he threatened me with torture, I reckon. I had foreseen some more traditional form of torture. Electric shocks, waterboard, matches under the nails, that sort of contrivance. Still, it's rather effective, nonetheless. Have to concede that to them. I didn't, for all that, start to wish I'd never been born, but I'd have been content to hand in the towel at the worst moments. Remembered those words scrawled in the toilet of that restaurant, over in Leeds that time. When I was there for the Nobel conference. If the bottom's fallen out of one's world, come to...where was it?...Chak's, that's it, come to Chak's and let the world fall out of one's bottom. Nowt funnier than wretchedness! Who was it said that? Can't remember. No worries.

*

When the warder comes with the oats, I tell him I'm not interested. He doesn't seem to mind too much, but he has a bit of a scream at me all the same. Who the fuck did I think I was? Who the fuck was I to waste his time like this? he mutters. Shouts. I tell him to be careful what he calls me. Fuck me! he shouts. I could have someone locked in the cooler for that! I leave it there. The more one treads on a turd the broader it becomes.

I feel so bad I decide that when the warder comes to fetch me, for the outside exercise, I'll tell him that I'm not well. I couldn't face it, and I know that when I'm called on to run like hell I won't be able to do it. Just too weak. I think I'd even find it difficult to walk, the state I'm in. In addition, I know that the woman next door stands a better chance on her own. If I went with her, it was all but certain I'd haul her down with me. Scuttle the break-out all round. In a word, it's an unavoidable sacrifice. Difficult, to be sure, but to act otherwise, I knew, would be madness.

It took both boldness and fortitude to make this decision – attributes I didn't think I had – but once I had I knew it was the correct one. Even if I'd be left alone here in the dark. Even if I'd be certain to be cross-examined as a result. For the Governor would realise that a break-out could not be hatched without a certain amount of co-ordination, and he would realise too that co-ordination needed a certain amount of communication. He had not been born last week. And he would know it was me in the next cell. He was sure to add two and two to make four. He wasn't an idiot. Even if he knew zilch about the code, or at least I reckoned he knew zilch about the code, I was sure he would come to me afterwards with his cross-examinations. Yet even if I saw all this with luminous clearness, I nonetheless felt content. I'd have done all I could do to ensure the success of the break-out. Of that I could be sure. I wouldn't receive a medal for it, but that didn't matter to me.

When the warder came to fetch me and I told him I wasn't fit for it, he seemed to understand. He warned me that there'd be no lunch, since the orderlies would all be out, but I said I believed I could handle that. That this would be OK. I didn't feel too famished for once, in truth. Afterwards I had a lie down on the bed for a while. In a state that hovered somewhere between unconsciousness and wakefulness. I'd had a turbulent time of it. Didn't know whether I would ever feel normal after all this. At one moment I believed I heard the warder hammer on the door with his metal cane. *Krrraannnn! Krrraannnn!* Had to remember it was all in the mind. Otherwise I'd have started to crawl over to the door. Like one of those bad dreams where one has to tell oneself all the while that it's all OK, don't fret, that it's no more than a dream.

In this state I lie on the old back in the cell, on the bed, drift into the tedious hours of the afternoon. I started to envision the events which would now run their course without me. The vans. How numerous would these be, how set out on the inside, who would travel in which? Whether or not there were different colour vans for the inmates, the orderlies, the warders, and the bosses. Or did the Colonel and his mates travel in a different kind of vehicle? A staff car, for instance? I tried to envision the excursion, the narrow and twisted road down which the vehicles travelled in their flotilla. Tried to envision how the inmates would react to each other in the back of the vans. Accustomed to solitude as these were, would all of them sit in absolute silence for the entire duration of the trek? Or would the inmates at once fall into conversation as if no behaviour could be more natural? I envisioned the arrival at the exercise field, as one and all streamed out of the vans, the inmates forced to shield their faces from the fierce sunshine as the warders herded them into clusters. I saw the Colonel stand at his lookout with his binoculars, the Governor strut about with an oversized Cohiba between his teeth – he looked for all the world like Churchill – and the warders who marched about with their Alsatians. As I envisioned the scene I made alterations here and there to increase the verisimilitude – the Colonel would be stood in the back of an armoured car, both to increase the extent of what he could see and to make him more mobile if the need arose – and as I did so I almost started to rue that I had remained in the cell. If I'd bitten the bullet and made a last effort, I said out loud, I would soon have been free! Then all in an instant I saw the two of us climb over the wall and into the concealed car, which roared off as soon as we were settled in our seats. We raced off, and vanished over the horizon, a trail of dust churned into the air behind us. I saw us draw over at a little riverside inn where we were issued with false I.D., civilian clothes, new boots, a Swiss forces' knife, some cash. We sat down to a hot meal then set off at once, this time in another vehicle, which would take us to a small farm near the border from where we would continue on horseback. We would cross the mountains, and when we came down on the other side we'd be free.

I saw us uncork a bottle of Prosecco over the border. I knew I did no more than add salt to the wound, but I found it hard to hold back, nonetheless. Yet I needed to tear back from these insane fantasies before I was driven over the brink. That route led to madness, I was sure of it. I needed to take a hold once more, whatever the cost. I sat vertical on the bed. Like a broom handle. Then over and over announced the bald truth, out loud, as I beat the mattress with two clenched fists.

There would be no bottle of Prosecco once over the border.

There would be no horse in attendance at the farm-house.

There would be no hot meal in the oven at the little riverside inn.

There would be no hero's welcome.

There would be no false I.D.

No civilian clothes.

No new boots.

No Swiss forces' knife.

No cash.

There would be no car there for us once over the wall.

There would be no outside exercise.

No vans.

No Alsatians.

There would be none of this. Not for me. Not for no-one. IT WAS ALL BULL! ALL BULL THE LOT OF IT! The tak-tak-tak, the communication from the other cells, the codes, the new codes, the break-out scheme, the exercise field, the allball. ALL BULL! ALL BULL FROM START TO FINISH! Just me stuck here in the dark, who invented the whole kit-and-caboodle, so I don't die of boredom. I cut out the dull bits, introduced some action, increased the tension, levied in the nice words. Like boldness. Like fortitude. When in actual fact boldness and fortitude have fuck all to do with it. Just need to be able to be on the move without so much as a backwards look. Like a clock. Just need to be able to survive. Like a rat.

*

Yet the rest is all true. The basics. The cell, the contents, the isolation, the dirt, the darkness, the mouse, the biscuits, the chocolate. The Governor and the rest of them too. Didn't invent that lot of crazed bastards, to be sure. Wish to God I had! What I told them about moles too. And the dreams. All too true. As far as I can tell, in this case. The truth is it's difficult to make a distinction between what's true and what isn't in here. In the dark. The silence. After a while one starts to tell oneself one's tale, so as to maintain one's feet on terra firma, so as to make sure the mind's active, then one starts to embellish matters a little, and before one knows it the whole business is out of hand. And one isn't trained for this sort of business, to be sure. Just tossed in, and not at the shallow end either, and after that it's sink or swim.

All that stuff about the tak-tak-tak from the wall. The codes, the inmates in the other cells, and so on. All that balls. You could call it a kind of necessitated fiction. Like in Wallace Stevens. I mean, it's hard to be alone like this, in the darkness. There's no-one else to talk to, so I have to invent, of course. Otherwise I'd be finished. So I start to talk as if there were someone there who listened, as I do now, still, can't avoid it. Then after a while one starts to believe it. You start to hear stuff. Add two and two and make five. The breakout scheme one could describe as wish fulfilment, I would think. But then what's not to like about that? No-one else will fulfil one's wishes in here, that's for sure. It's a case of DIY or not at all. I see no alternative, in this case.

*

The warder came in. Told me to shut that mouth of mine. I didn't even realise that it wasn't shut, but that would seem to have been the case. Must have lost control and started to talk out loud. Just shut that mouth, he said, otherwise someone else will have to shut it. I knew what he meant. Curious choice of words he makes at times. As I do, no doubt, in the effort to be succinct. Effort to economise on notebooks. Two of his friends came in a few moments afterwards. One of them carried in a chair, a bulb, the other came with a biro and notebooks. Somewhat astonished, I asked if these were for me. The warder answered in the affirmative. Whatever for, for God's sake? I asked him. Orders, he said. Verboseness was not one of his faults. The men twisted the bulb into its socket, switched it on and left. Without so much as a word. Like breeds like, as is often said. I could see its flicker from behind the blindfold. It occurred to me that I could have asked them if I was now allowed to take it off. The blindfold. No-one had said so, but it seemed fair to assume, nonetheless. If I was to make use of the notebooks and the biro, which it would be fair to assume that I was, then I'd need to take the blindfold off, wouldn't I? Otherwise I would not be able to use the biro and notebooks, nor would I be able to use the bulb to see with. So all that work on the door, on the hole, had been a waste of time! No, I reasoned. Not a total waste of time. I could now at least tell when I was watched. When not watched. And I could therefore walk about the cell at will, unobserved, if I wanted to. Which at the moment I didn't. I eased off the blindfold and threw it down on the bed. I looked at the cadeaux. The chair, the bulb, the biro, the notebooks. It all seemed too fantastical to be true, like some evanescent enchantment out of a wonder tale, and I feared that if I were to reach out and touch them, these items were sure to dissolve, like cloud-covered castles. It also seemed odd to be without the blindfold. It was the first time I had removed it in toto, so that for once it did not encircle the neck, like a scarf, or a noose.

*

Krrraannnnn! Krrraannnn! The warder. With the bread and broth. *Krrraannnn!* I walk over to the door, beneath the bulb's flicker. Push in the mess tin. Hear him ladle the broth in. Push it back. With the bread. Thin lettuce and water mixture, as is usual. A little salt to the taste. I wolf it down, as usual. Save the bread. Put it in the little recess to the left of the door. I make a visit to the sink to wash, when all of a sudden I remember the little dormouse, wonder how he is. When I reach the sink I see it all before me. It seems that he has tried to bolt down the sink hole, where his head and most of his torso are now hidden. He must have acted as a kind of live cork, as he became stuck in there, as he made his break-out bid, while the faucet continued to trickle onto his backside, in the end to drown him. It was a slow death, to be sure. His tail sticks out, stiff like wire, into the air, where it has set in the form of a

?

I wonder whether his little life unravelled before him at the moment of death. As it's said to do in humans. With both hands I haul him out, tail first. It is difficult, for his torso is stiff with death. When I've succeeded, I take him to the far corner of the room. Shove him into one of the cracks I've uncovered. Cover it with a clean sheet. Then I sit on the bed and mumble a little devotion for him. Shed a tear for him. He deserved a better owner, I think. Please God that he bears me no ill will.

As I mutter these devotions, think these matters over, I hold a firm hand over the mouth. Just to check I haven't started to talk out loud once more. Better safe than rue it. The Governor hasn't done that for me, even now. Given me the licence to talk out loud. But then I wouldn't want them to hear me utter the little devotion for the dormouse, whatever. This is between me and him. Or me and her. Never did work out which sex it is. Was. Don't know how one tells with mice. And I wouldn't want them to think I'd lost the old marbles, either. Won't let them have the satisfaction. Even if I am. Have.

I sit on the bed. Knees at 45°, elbows on knees, head between hands. Think of the mouse, the biro, the notebooks, the bulb, the hours of dusk that stretch before me. I envision that all of a sudden I stand and walk over to the table. Sit down. Pen in hand. Take out the notebook. I think about what I should write, now that I have the materials. How should I frame the statement? Could kick off with how I don't know how I arrived here, and don't know what I'm here for, or for how extended a stretch of time. An account of the warder, the room, the diurnal routine. Kick off with the mundanities, I think, to make a start. Write down some of the matters one runs over in one's head. Flush it all out. Or should I write about the behavioural habits of moles? That's what the Governor will look forward to, after all. But then I know damn all about the behavioural habits of moles. Not in the literal sense, to be sure.

Then I stall. See the catch. Put down the notebook.

What the Governor wants from me is a confession. That was made clear. And if I write so much as a word he'll twist it round in his hands in a thousand different directions, until he's convinced himself that he has one. That's the little trick he now tries to lure me with. I see it at once. Clear as a mountain stream. He tries to deceive me with the illusion that he's conceded to a modest demand, but in actual fact he has delivered into these mole hands the means with which the fate of this mole will be sealed, once and for all. Devious. If that's the case, so be it. He can stuff his bollocks notebooks. He can shove them into the inner recesses of his arse for all I care.

I resolved not to make use of the notebooks that I had been furnished with. Nor of the bulb. I switched it off. Could be I didn't have the licence, but I switched it off all the same. I resolved too to talk to no-one from now on. I would talk neither to the orderlies, nor to the warder, nor to the Governor. Nor to the Colonel, nor to the Lieutenant. Nor to Gore. I would start a silence strike. That would teach them. Like that, no-one would ever extract a confession from me. I saw too that one should not even talk to oneself. Not even in the head. For it had become more and more difficult to know whether or not I could retain these ideas of mine inside the mind, and not blurt them out loud. That much had been demonstrated with the warder's visit. And if one talked to oneself, in the head, or rather believed one talked to oneself, in the head, and in actual fact one talked out loud, then what was there to hinder them, the Governor would utter the command and a hidden recorder would be secreted in the cell at once. And once he had a record of the words, he could use them in the same manner in which he intended to use the written word.

So I resolved to talk no more. I couldn't be sure it would work. But all the same, I was determined to have a bash. Nowt ventured, nowt won, as is often said in Leeds. That's what one has to tell oneself, to be sure.

In the head, hands over mouth, I run over an A-Z of writers. To stick on the bookshelf. Next to the table. One last time, in the head, as a kind of farewell. For I won't need these sorts of hobbies from now on. Could be, another time, I'll even have a bit of a read. Now I've the bulb. But no, on reflection I think I'd better not. One must hand oneself over to the silence. To the dark. I do the best to make it the same as that with which I started. But I can't be sure. A lot has kicked off since then and remembrances aren't what I'd call reliable. If I'd have written it all down from the start, I could have flicked back over the book to check. But I haven't. Can't. Here then.

Aristotle	
Balzac	
Chekov	
Dickinson	
Eliot	
Faulkner	
Goethe	Mmm. Should be able to do better than that. Yes.
Gide	
Hawthorne	
Ionesco	
James	
Kafka	A bird went in search of a net.
Lawrence	
Mandelstam	Old connoisseur in the science of farewells.
Nabokov	
Ovid	

Proust
Quintilian

Rabelais

Swift

Tolstoi *The Convict*. Got it!

Uris ?????????
Verlaine
Wells

Xenocrates
Yeats Cast a deaf ear on life, on death.
Horseman, ride on.

Zola

Exeter-London-Wivenhoe, 1994-2020

Afterword

It was my father who first drew my attention to the story of Edith Bone, which he had come across while reading Anthony Storr's *Solitude* (1988), that strange and compelling study of the benefits of solitude, especially for creative work. Storr records how Dr Edith Bone, a distinguished linguist, was arrested in Hungary in 1949 and accused of being a British agent. Though imprisoned in the most terrible conditions, she refused to sign a false confession, and kept herself sane by inventing numerous techniques, from reciting and translating poetry, to making inventories of the languages she knew, to going on imaginary walks. It was sometime later that I began to consider writing a short novel loosely based on this story, which I first drafted in the 1990s, then abandoned as I felt I couldn't find the right form in which to tell it. In truth, I am a poor novelist, as the poet in me always wants to find a linguistic form which matches the subject matter of the world I am writing about, and the novel is less open to this than poetry, perhaps because as a genre it is generally more conservative, perhaps because it is generally longer. I never abandoned the novel completely, however, but kept revisiting it, never quite giving up hope of finding a successful means to release its story. After numerous false starts and metamorphoses, too many to enumerate here, in 2018, while researching *The Penguin Book of Oulipo* (2019), I came across the method I would finally settle on. I had known about Oulipo's technique, which they call the "prisoner's constraint", for some time – to save space a prisoner writes with only those letters of the alphabet without either ascenders or descenders, a, c, e, i, m, n, o, r, s, u, v, w, x, and z – and I realised that only the shortest and most cryptic texts could be pulled off with such a hard constraint, but in reading Oulipo's *L'Abécédaire provisoirement définitif* (*The Provisionally Definitive ABC*, 2014) I came across for the first time Michèle Audin's loosening of this constraint, wherein ascenders are allowed. Letting in the letters b, d, f, h, k, l, and t, and thereby considerably expanding the palette, liberating new possibilities of expression, I knew I'd finally found my constraint. I set about rewriting the book without descenders in a whirl of enthusiasm, which I hadn't known for years, in early 2019, and completed a first draft in just over 53 days. Weirdly, the final revisions to the book were completed under the UK Covid-19 lockdown, in spring 2020, a difficult and painful period for the whole country, but during which many people found the enforced solitude led to moments of personal creativity and breakthrough, an experience which is strangely echoed in the story adapted here.

When I received the first proofs of the book in November 2020 I was in for a mild shock. The font I had used while writing the book was Arial, where the "f" and italic "f" are both without descenders. But the book, in keeping with Grand Iota's house style, was set in Georgia. Here the "f" is as with Arial, but the italic "*f*" protrudes below the line, so breaking the constraint, and the same thing happens with the numerals 3, 4, 5, 7 and 9. In a flash, I saw all the patient work I had put in unravel in an instant. I got in touch with the publisher to see if there was a way to remedy the situation. Could we use underline instead of italics? Could we change the font for the numerals? To cut a long story short, in the end it was decided to do without the italic "f" but otherwise to leave things as they were. And after sleeping on it, I came to see the aberrant numerals as part of the fabric of the book. The novel, after all, is *about* disobedience, at one level, and here this is enacted at the level of the constraint. Oulipo talk of the "clinamen", a term derived from Lucretius describing the swerve of atoms that fall in otherwise straight lines, and for Oulipo this denotes a breaking of the constraint for aesthetic reasons. From this angle, while the book I had written in Arial fully obeys the constraint, this newly-introduced "clinamen" can be seen as a flaw that both breaks the constraint but also, in doing so, makes the book more human in its imperfection, and definitively finishes it as it does so – somewhat like the blank chapter in Perec's *Life A User's Manual*, or the crack in Duchamp's *Large Glass*, which was broken during transport after being exhibited at the Brooklyn Museum in 1926.

Philip Terry, November 2020

Also available from grand**IOTA**

APROPOS JIMMY INKLING
Brian Marley
978-1-874400-73-8 318pp

WILD METRICS
Ken Edwards
978-1-874400-74-5 244pp

BRONTE WILDE
Fanny Howe
978-1-874400-75-2 158pp

THE GREY AREA
Ken Edwards
978-1-874400-76-9 328pp

PLAY, A NOVEL
Alan Singer
978-1-874400-77-6 268pp

THE SHENANIGANS
Brian Marley
978-1-874400-78-3 220pp

SEEKING AIR
Barbara Guest
978-1-874400-79-0 218pp

JOURNEYS ON A DIME: SELECTED STORIES
Toby Olson
978-1-874400-80-6 300pp

Production of this book has been made possible with the help of the following individuals and organisations who subscribed in advance:

Peter Bamfield
Chris Beckett
Lillian Blakey
Andrew Brewerton
Ian Brinton
Jasper Brinton
Peter Brown
Mark Callan
Robert Caserio
John Cayley
cris cheek
Claire Crowther
Rachel DuPlessis
Ian Durant
Allen Fisher/Spanner
Nancy Gaffield
Susan Gevirtz
Jim Goar
Giles Goodland
Penny Grossi
John Hall
Andrew Hamilton
Robert Hampson
Peter Hodgkiss
Peter Hughes
Kristoffer Jacobson
Howard Jones
Steve Lake
Alison Lambert
Stacey Levine
James McDonald
Richard Makin
Michael Mann
Askold Melnyczuk
Joe Milazzo
John Muckle
Richie Nice
Jim O'Brien
Françoise Palleau
Sean Pemberton
Dennis Phillips
Pablo Seoane Rodríguez
David Rose
Lou Rowan
James Russell
Maurice Scully
Steven Seidenberg
Valerie Soar
Lloyd Swanton
Eileen Tabios
Robert Vas Dias
visual associations
John Wilkinson
Tyrone Williams
Tamar Yoseloff
anon x 2

www.grandiota.co.uk